Genie and the Ghost

A COZY PARANORMAL GENIE AND ADRIANA DARLING MURDER MYSTERY

CARMEN RADTKE

ADAMANTINE BOOKS

Copyright © 2023 by Carmen Radtke

All rights reserved.

No portion of this book may be reproduced in any form without written permission from the publisher or author, except as permitted by U.S. copyright law.

Paperback ISBN 978-1-9162410-7-7

Cover design by DLR Coverdesigns

www.carmenradtke.com

Dedication

This book would not have been written without you. Yes, you.

If you're one of my loyal readers – thank you, from the bottom of my heart.

If you're new to my books, welcome. I hope you'll stay.

There have been more moments than I care to admit where I felt scared and wondered if this will be the book that I can't finish, the one that tells me to maybe do something else.

But all it takes is one short message, one word of appreciation, or a review telling me that my books have given someone else joy, provided distraction, or made them see things in a new light.

For all that, I thank you.

We're in this together.

Contents

Cast of Characters

The family

Genie Darling, quick-witted jewelry designer who's in for the surprise of her life

Adriana Darling, Genie's great-great-aunt, a vivacious flapper, who's making the most of her new lease of life as a ghost

Aimée Darling Hepner, Genie's Francophile mother, sadly oblivious to Adriana's presence

Tony Hepner, Aimée's new husband

Cleo, the tabby cat who's under Adriana's spell

The town people

Primrose and Dahlia Schuyler, a couple of mature sisters who run the local museum and most other things in Cobblewood Cove

George Schuyler, their nephew, who has a soft spot for Aimée

Huggins, their elderly butler

Fred Ward, who fills his retirement with volunteer jobs at the library and the museum

Daphne Mills, head librarian

Jolene Ortega, unflappable woman of all trades

Matthew Blake, her second cousin twice removed, art and museum security expert

Jonathan Harewood, the most eligible bachelor in town

Bert, a handyman

Miss Lola, hairdresser and fountain of gossip

Police officer Hank Newby, Jolene's other cousin

Police officer Tilda Ramos, his partner on the job

Petey, a parrot

Fifi and Groucho, dogs with vital information

CHAPTER ONE

"Watch out!" A shrill shriek followed the order. I slammed the door to the cloak room or what I'd taken for the cloak room shut.

"I'm so sorry." Dahlia Schuyler, a slight septuagenarian with white hair piled up becomingly on top of her head and a black dress that put my own blue affair from the sales at Macy's to shame, peered at me with concern. "I should have put a warning sign. Not that Petey would ever do any harm, but the sweet boy can be a bit excitable."

Indeed. Not to mention that parrot droppings might not exactly be the thing to greet you guests with at a party, or rather soiree as the invitation had stated, I thought.

"I hope he didn't scare you." My hostess gave me a probing look, as if to gauge the extent of the damage the shock might have done me.

"Not at all. I like animals." I hovered, my coat over my arms. It would have been wiser to stay in line to hand the garment to the elderly manservant at the door, but since I planned to spend as little time as

1

possible without being impolite I'd thought it wise to find out where the coats were kept. Or in this case, weren't.

Dahlia raised her hand and the manservant relieved me of my burden. "If you'll allow me."

I graciously nodded to him and followed my hostess to the ball room where the main action took place.

As soon as I entered, a gasp escaped me. I'd never set foot in here before or even spent more than a few weeks in my ancestor's hometown of Cobblewood Cove, but ten foot ceilings, crystal chandeliers and period furniture did not feature in the itself not too shabby Darling villa three quarters of a mile away. Everything here was in incredible taste and probably the real deal, as far as I could tell.

"You must be the niece." Thin hands mottled with age clasped mine and a powdered cheek briefly came close enough for a fake kiss. "I don't know if you remember me. I'm Primrose Schuyler, Dahlia's sister. I'm sorry I forgot your name. It comes with the years, I'm afraid." Apart from the golden hues of her coiffure she resembled her sister to a striking extent.

Her laughter held a nervous edge. It must be irksome for any woman to admit you're temporarily at a loss, especially when you and your sister practically run the social register. Not to mention the local museum, which was the reason I'd sacrificed an evening with a good book and a cat on my lap. But the Schuyler sisters were too nice to poke fun at. Rich and kind was a rare combination in my experience.

I gave her my best smile, one that conveyed admiration and respect as well as a touch of familiarity. After all, they'd once plied me with lemonade and a bandage for my skinned knees after I'd overestimated my rollerblading skills. "Great-niece, and it's Genevieve, but please call me Genie. Everybody does." I had my mother to thank for a name hardly anyone could pronounce, an accent and vocabulary that were all over the place or rather map, just like I had to thank her for this evening.

"Genie. I'm so sorry about your great-aunt. You remind me of her." Primrose sighed.

So did I. My great-aunt Lottie, who'd recently gone to her just re-wards, had been as eccentric as they come, with a passion for quilting. She'd even created her own special funeral quilt which she was buried with. It must have taken her months, if not years, to hand-stitch satin birds and squirrels onto the tiny squares but then she'd lived to a ripe old age.

Although the house had technically come to my mother when I was little, nobody would have dreamt of turfing out my great-aunt. Or her acreage of quilting materials and tapestries (another passion of hers). It would have been cruel, apart from the fact that my parents, and I with them, changed countries every couple of years. My mother had never lived in the house since her wedding day, and moving Lottie in had been both an act of generosity and a way to have someone who loved the place taking care of it.

Still, as fond as everyone had been of Lottie, I hoped I didn't really take after her when it came to obsession with handicraft. As much as I loved creating my intricate jewelry, I had more going on in my life.

"How is your dear mother? And you, Genie, are you going to stay in Cobblewood Cove? So nice to have some young blood around."

The elderly manservant shuffled past with a silver tray full of stuffed mushrooms and fish balls. My mouth watered. Mine wasn't the only one. I could see the other guests help themselves to the food as soon

3

as it appeared. Most of them were past retirement age. Their conversation seemed to consist of golfing, stocks, and grandchildren, going by the snippets I snatched up, but they had excellent hand-to-mouth coordination when it came to my favorite appetizers.

They'd inspired the food blog I'd started during my college years. Everything I rated had to stack up against the local delicatessen. A tough call, since Pierre, the owner of Butler's Pantry, set the bar sky-high.

I tried not to drool. "My mother sends her regards. She's on her honeymoon."

"Is she going to live here?" Primrose pulled me over to a sofa.

"Probably not. But I'll stay at least long enough to sort through everything that might be right for your exhibition."

Cobblewood Cove, or Prescott Village as it had been called for its two first decades, until the namesake was found out to sympathize with the British during the War of 1812, sat halfway between Boston and New York. It had now been decided to honor its not very illustrious past (apart from the infamous Prescott) with an event at the local museum.

Since the Darlings had come here not long after the Schuylers, when the ink on the Declaration of Independence was still drying, our contributions were eagerly awaited, even if they only consisted of moth-eaten clothes, an old chamberpot or two, and faded letters. At least that's what I supposed I would find. Our attic was crammed with trunks and boxes that themselves were covered with quilts and tapestries.

I didn't want to accuse my mother of scheduling her honeymoon with the intention on dumping the whole affair into my lap, but after ten years of widowhood the timing did seem a little suspicious.

"And then you're off again?" Primrose seemed genuinely disappointed as she waved over one of the two men who reduced the average age in the room to under 60.

They were a study in contrast, with one slender and blond and blue-eyes and the other one broad-shouldered, with dark hair and dark eyes.

I had to admit that they were both personable enough, with the fair one Primrose had beckoned almost too handsome.

"Jonathan, have you met Genie Darling?" She left us standing as she joined her sister and another group.

His eyes held an amused twinkle as he handed me a glass of champagne. "You'd probably be rich if you had a dime for every 'out of the bottle' joke."

"I'd be rolling in it," I said.

He chuckled. "I think our families go way back. Harewood? Ring a bell?"

"Should it? I'm not really that well-versed in the old family lore. But aren't all the old families somehow acquainted?"

"True enough. Except for you. How did you escape Cobblewood Cove?" He steered me even further away from the food.

"My dad worked for a company that sent him to a new city and new country every few years. That's probably why my mother married him. She wanted to go live in a Paris that wasn't located in Oneida County."

He laughed at my wit, a point in his favor.

I sipped my drink and tried to make my way to the nibbles before I had more champagne on an empty stomach.

Sadly, I had underestimated everyone's interest in me, or rather in my absent mother. My path seemed littered with well-meaning, well-dressed, well-heeled people who liked nothing better than to reminisce about days I hadn't been around for and events happening long before I was born.

My stomach growled.

"Have some of these." Those two wonderful words were accompanied by a plate with, yes, fish balls and stuffed mushrooms among other assorted nibbles.

"You might have just saved my life," I said before I crammed a fish ball into my mouth.

The name didn't do them justice. They were sphere-shaped morsels of pure, melt-in-the-mouth bliss. The recipe was rumored to have come over with a French Huguenot by the moniker of Pierre Bouteillier, who'd been fleeing persecution long before Cobblewood Cove was founded.

The exact ingredients were still kept secret by the chef and the whole town worried whenever the current Pierre had so much as a sniffle, not just because he was such a likable guy, but also because so far he was the last chef in the family, and childless. That did not bode well for a catering company where recipes were passed down from generation to generation, in a town where family trees and inheritance established your position on the totem pole.

Not that newcomers weren't welcome; they were. They just were encouraged to keep a low profile until they'd been around long enough to earn their stripes after a mere four or five decades or so. The only exception to the rule was a reclusive investor who'd purchased the most prestigious property in the area, a Palladian-style mansion on top of the cliff leading down to the cove.

His ready acceptance came thanks to his wealth, although the youth of the town probably thought otherwise.

The small sandy beach leading to the water had long been the local hotspot for romance and parties away from the parents. Said millionaire had spoiled the fun with floodlights everywhere that blinded everyone within a mile if so much as a dog ran across the sand. Now, the cove was only used during the day, by small children playing in the sand and jumping off the jetty. An ice-cream van and a lemonade stall offered refreshments until the sunset.

I had fond memories of that place, in both iterations. I had long since grown out of the fun of drinking around a campfire or a few private moments with a boy, but Cobblewood Cove had lost an attraction when it gained this particular resident.

The dark haired thirty-something man who'd supplied me with the food probably belonged to the normal category of newcomer. Where Jonathan had first been claimed by a group of elderly golf enthusiasts which now merged with gardening lovers, he could move freely.

I devoured another fish ball before I remembered my manners. "I'm not usually this greedy."

"As long as you don't spoil your appetite, Genie, dear." Primrose appeared by my side. "Dinner will be served in half an hour. Not on the Wedgwood, in case you were wondering." She'd directed the last sentence at my hero, but added for my benefit, "Matthew Blake has been kind enough to value our collections for insurance purposes. He'll do the same with everything on loan to the museum."

7

Was that a worry line between her delicately arched brows?

"I'm sure there's no need to be concerned about anything," I said.

"You're right. It's still such a relief to have an expert at hand."

Matt interpreted my puzzled look correctly. "I usually do appraisals when it comes to large ticket items that might tempt people. And call me Matt."

Primrose lowered her voice. "We had to tell one donor that their Fabergé brooch was nothing but paste, but there are other objects. Matt made us update the security system."

"You could spot it was a fake?" My interest grew.

"There's telltale signs." He gave a modest shrug.

"I know. I'm a silversmith." I touched my chandelier earrings. "I mostly do modern uptakes on Art Deco and Egyptian Revival pieces."

Sadly, we did not sit together at dinner, but with Jonathan by my side, I couldn't complain. He regaled me with stories about art fairs and stores that might be interested in my merchandise.

I started to enjoy myself, although the wine to go with five courses might have had something to do with it. But I was also tired, and I had promised myself an early start to tackle the hoarded relics in the attic. I yawned as we finally were allowed to rise from the table.

"Thank you for a splendid evening." I air-kissed Dahlia and Primrose in the correct manner which had taken me ages to perfect.

"Are you leaving already? I'll take you to your car." Jonathan seemed genuinely disappointed to see me go.

I caught a glimpse of Matt as he passed us.

He gave me a little grin.

I grinned back.

"I'm walking," I said to Jonathan. "It'll clear my head."

"Are you sure?"

I nodded. "It's only a few blocks."

"But you have a car? Or we could send you home in ours." Dahlia asked.

"Thanks, but I really enjoy a stroll." They did not appear convinced, but let me go my merry way.

The Schuyler's lived in a red brick mansion at one of the corners of the four streets surrounding the cobble-stoned square. All the front windows afforded them a view of the peacock fountain - with good reason. The fountain had been generously donated by one of their ancestors.

Only the Harewoods lived in a taller red brick building, on the opposite side of the square. Lesser inhabitants made do with clapboard villas or smaller brick houses. The lack of uniformity added to the visual appeal.

I lingered a little. The half moon cast its weak light through a cloud but there were a few stars visible in the night sky, and the street lamps were just bright enough to add a movie-set charm to the scenery.

The April air held a touch of frost. I put up my coat collar as I turned around the corner. One hundred yards ahead lay the Darling villa, all three ivy-covered floors of it.

The bells of the Presbyterian church struck eleven.

Something behind my back alarmed me a split second before I felt a tug at my purse strings and a heavy shove. I swung my leg backwards, kicking out with all my might, while I used my handbag to roundhouse whoever attacked me. My foot made satisfying contact with a leg, and I heard a yelp.

Unfortunately I'd underestimated my own momentum. I stumbled forward.

"Are you okay?" Strong hands helped me right myself. The patter of footsteps told me that my assailant was fleeing the scene of the crime. To make doubly sure, I cast a quick glance at my supporter's pant legs. No signs of a kick.

To be honest, anything else would have been a miracle. The nice man who gently held my arms could easily have been my grandfather and weighed around the same as me. Still, I had to check.

He peered at me with deep concern. "It's a good thing I left the party right after you. If only my eyes were what they used to be."

"The party?"

"I sat at the end of the table. It's Fred Ward and I live one street over from you."

Now I recognized him. I wasn't normally this slow on the uptake, but then this had been my first encounter with a mugger in the night-time. Or any other hour.

"Did you recognize the person?" I asked, although I held out little hope in this faint illumination.

"He had a mask on, at least I think so. I was more concerned with you, I'm afraid."

"I'm glad you were." I meant it. Without him, I might have taken a nasty tumble. Also, my attacker might easily have taken down my gallant hero.

Fred offered to carry my bag for me, like the old-fashioned gentle-man he seemed. "Please remember me to your mom," he said. "She used to come around to see my sister every day, just before I left for college."

It could have been my imagination by I thought I'd heard a slight tremble in his voice. At least I knew why he was so concerned about me. Fred Ward, like many others, had been sweet on my mother.

My hands shook as I let myself into the house. I headed straight for the living room, with only the hallway light on. I flung my coat onto the rack, sank onto the armchair and kicked off my shoes.

"Ouch!" The cry startled me. I hit the light switch and stared at the face of a young woman I'd never seen in my life, sitting bolt upright on the sofa.

CHAPTER TWO

M y mouth fell open. The logical thing was to call the police and tell them I had an intruder.

"I'll ring up the police." The woman glared daggers at me, not a mean feat considering she looked like a vintage glamour girl with her huge baby-blue eyes, silver flapper dress and wavy blonde hair to complete the look.

Her reaction seemed genuine. Maybe my dear departed great-aunt had given her a key? But then wouldn't she have known that said Lottie had moved on to the great craft store in the sky or whatever lay ahead for her?

Also, Blondie would have heard about my arrival. I didn't flatter myself, but you don't have roots dating back a gazillion generations in a place like Cobblewood Cove without people talking about your return.

Her eyes narrowed. "Hey, why are you wearing my sister's earrings? Planning to go on the lam with them?" She drew herself up to her full height, which was about the same as mine.

I'd always thought the expression 'shudders ran down my spine' as a cliche, but that's exactly how I felt. Here I was, confronted with an obviously deranged stranger, in my mother's house, after I'd just escaped a mugging attempt. And they said small town life was dull.

I slowly reached for my purse with my phone inside. "I made those earrings myself. There's my card on the table. Genevieve Darling, jewelry designer and silversmith."

Those earrings were among my finest creations, inspired by old family pictures. My full name was Genevieve Darling Hepner, but my mother's maiden name sounded better for my business.

"Cut the baloney. Your fella given you the bum's rush? That's why you're hiding out here?" The blonde beauty chuckled, obviously enjoying every moment of this crazy exchange.

"Very funny," I said. "I, or rather my family, happen to own this house, so whatever your game is, it's over. I won't press charges, but I really want you to leave."

"Hold it, lady, I'm not a sucker. I was born in this house, so you scram." She looked around more closely, at the faded wallpaper dating back to pre-war days (the Darlings liked to stock up on things they loved in case they were discontinued, which meant that despite repapering every couple of decades, the pattern stayed unchanged) and the slightly younger pictures on the wall.

In one corner hung a framed, hand-drawn family tree that had suffered from hanging next to an open fireplace. Nobody would have dreamt of getting rid of it just because half of it was soot-blackened.

13

Likewise, nobody would have thought of having it professionally re-stored. It would have destroyed the authenticity. Or maybe my ancestors simply forgot because who looked at family trees, except for snobs?

She pointed at my great-aunt's latest tapestry, a bucolic scene with sheep and herd dogs in garish colors, thanks to the artist's cataracts. "What on earth is that?"

"You get used to it. Or rather, you won't, because you're going."

"There should be a mirror in the same place. What have you done with it? Pawned it?"

"There used to be one," I said, with rising confusion. "How do you know that?"

Cleo, my mother's tabby cat whose care was the one responsibility I enjoyed, selected this moment to stroll into the room. She'd probably finished her nap on my bed, which came after her beauty sleep on my work chair. She gave a loud purr as she saw the stranger who had now decided to recline elegantly on the sofa.

Only, where said piece of furniture sagged a little when I did the same, nothing moved. Weird.

Cleo and the woman gazed at each other.

"Hello, kitty-cat," the intruder said and patted the sofa next to her.

Cleo jumped up and snuggled into the woman's lap.

My mouth went dry. I probed my head. Had I bumped it during my earlier tussles? Because a concussion was the only thing that made sense now.

Otherwise, I'd just seen a cat sink onto a sofa, right through a human body, before it became solid again. It had only been a fleeting impression, but one that made me doubt my sanity.

"You're looking awfully pale," my uninvited guest said. "Too much hooch? Do you need a doctor?"

"Maybe. Do you have a number?" I reached for my phone.

She stared at it. "What's that?"

I put it aside. "Maybe aspirin will be enough."

She sat up with a curious expression and took my phone. Or rather, she didn't. Try as she might, she couldn't pick it up. Her fingers became translucent whenever she tried.

A gulp escaped me.

"What's your name?" I asked her. "We haven't introduced ourselves."

She sighed. "You're not from around here, are you? I'm Adriana Darling and everybody has heard of me."

Oh so casually, I strolled over to the framed family tree. There, in one corner, I could make out a faint Adr, before the soot covered the rest. With a bit of imagination, three numbers underneath were decipherable too. I grabbed onto the mantelpiece for support.

"What date is it?"

She rolled her eyes.

"I mean, what year do we have?" Please, I prayed silently, let me be wrong.

Another eye-roll. "1929. What did you expect?"

I had my answer, and I didn't like it one bit. How do you tell someone she's your great-great-aunt and she's also dead? Because if my eyes and her words were right, I was dealing with a ghost.

CHAPTER THREE

Adriana poked my phone. It didn't budge. "Is that a trick thing?"

"I need a drink." I rarely had more than a glass of wine or two, but this called for something stronger. And luckily the recently departed Lottie had left behind a battery of booze. That is - was she even dead? Were there more Darling women lurking around, waiting for their big moment?

No. I calmed down. For one thing, my late great-aunt had been on my father's side. She had been a dear, but not a Darling. Considering that Adriana was my first ghost in my 32 years on earth, it appeared unlikely that a herd of my ancestors lay in ambush.

If I remembered correctly from old books and movies, ghosts were souls unable to cross over, because they had one unfinished task left. Or something like that.

Okay. I poured myself a brandy. I'd figure out what Adriana needed to accomplish, help her do it, and wave her off into the sunset, or the afterlife. How hard could it be?

"Do you have giggle water?" Adriana had given up on my phone and inspected the liquor cabinet with mounting delight. "Now that's a sight for sore eyes. Are you chummy with a bootlegger? Not even my sister's sweetheart could lay his hands on this lot, and his daddy used to have a finger in every pie."

Giggle-water? I mentally face-palmed. She meant champagne. I should have been able to translate that, but the day had been exhausting and the night even more so.

Regretfully, I shook my head. "How about a snifter for you too?"

She pulled a face. "If that's the best you can do."

I felt a pang of guilt as I put the tumbler in front of her.

Cleo stared at me with reproachful eyes as her new friend struggled to pick up the glass and failed, again and again.

"Sorry," I mouthed.

"What's going on?" Adriana's voice took on a frightened edge.

There was no easy way to put this. "You can't move the glass or my phone, because technically you don't exist. It's not 1929. That was almost a century ago."

She shook her perfectly styled head in bewilderment. "Applesauce. That's screwy."

"It is." I gently touched her shoulder, or would have had, if I could have made contact. Instead, I felt nothing under my fingers.

She swayed.

Instinctively, I wafted the brandy under her nose.

She sucked in the aroma. A serene smile spread over her face. "That's better."

I held the brandy under her nose again, and her smile grew even wider. "Bottoms up." She giggled.

I sniffed at the brandy. The smell was strong. I took a sip. Even stronger, but far from making me giggle or sway. Fabulous. I didn't simply have a ghost situation, I'd also made her tipsy.

"Can you lie down?" I asked. "I think we could all do with some rest, and we'll talk about things in the morning."

Her head lolled as she nodded. Obediently, she followed Cleo to the sofa.

I spread a quilt over the two, or maybe just over the cat, and took myself off to bed as well.

I woke up with a start. That was the craziest, yet most realistic dream I'd had in ages.

"Good morning," a voice sang into my ears. Something soft touched my cheek. My eyes flew open to find myself face to face with the cat and Adriana. My alarm clock told me it was technically still my bedtime so I pulled the duvet over my head. It would be tough enough to get a grip on the situation after I'd had my regular eight hours.

It didn't work. Tiny claws tugged at my cover.

"We're hungry," Adriana said.

"We?"

"It's not my fault. I can't help it." A slight wobble in her voice tugged at my heartstrings. It wasn't her doing that I tended to be grumpy if I had too little sleep and too big problems. Or that she was here at all. I rolled out of bed and wrapped myself into my bathrobe.

"Cleo wants fish. With lots of sauce. And a piece of bacon." Adriana's face took on a dreamy expression. "Extra crisp, with a side of pancakes or waffles."

"For Cleo?"

"For me. She just wants the fish. And bacon."

"She's supposed to have raw meat." As soon as I said it, I realized how weird it was to discuss the cat's menu with Adriana.

"She says the beef tastes like you looked when you read that letter last week."

I stumbled over my own feet. She must mean the notice my soon to be ex-landlord had given my best friend Jilly and me on the lease of our shared flat and studio, on the farthest outskirts that could technically still count as New York. That's where we created Darling Jewelry and Pepper's Pots.

Or used to create them. I'd known it was coming, but it had still been a shock to see it in writing. All my precious silversmithing tools, the semi-precious stones and enamel I worked with were currently boxed up and kept in a small storage unit. Jilly's oven, clay and other paraphernalia took up the rest of the storage space. We'd decided to think over our best way forward while I visited Cobblewood Cove and she spent a couple of weeks with her parents in Seattle.

But how could Adriana, or the cat know?

"Cleo and I had a long chin last night, didn't we, sweetheart?" A barely visible finger stroked a feline head. A blissful sigh rewarded her efforts.

How was that even possible? "You can touch Cleo? And talk to her?"

"She said a lot of swell things about you." Adriana gave me a dimpled smile. "I'm sure she'll be even happier with you if you feed us."

The cat wove around her legs as we headed to the kitchen. I rubbed my temple. I'd figure out the logistics later.

Adriana's nostrils flared as I opened the fridge. If inhaling the scent of brandy made her tipsy, maybe smelling fried bacon would make her feel sated?

"Don't forget Cleo," she said as I dropped two rashers into the frying pan.

I added a tiny piece.

"More," she said. "It's her favorite." She blew the cat a kiss and Cleo miaowed.

When we were all full and I had enough caffeine in my system to allow me to think straight, I pulled out a notepad. On the first page, I made a quick pencil sketch of my guest.

Drawing helped me think, and if I wanted to speed my great-great-aunt on her way, I needed information. I compared my drawing with the original. I'd captured the innocent air that made her vulnerable despite the sophisticated appearance.

Pencil poised, I began my interrogation. "What's the last thing you remember?"

She gave a discreet little burp. "Oops, I overdid the bacon smelling a bit. I remember you saying, what's the last thing you remember."

Great. A ghost who also wanted to be a comedian.

"Before meeting me," I said.

She nibbled her lip. "We'd been to this new speakeasy in Boston. Everybody said it was the bee's knees, and boy, were they right. They had a three man band and dancing and all the good stuff from straight over the border. I wore my new dress. Spiffy, isn't it?" She twirled. Her dress shimmered like moonlight on the lake.

Something stung in my eyes. She looked so happy caught up in her memories, and so beautiful, and alive.

"And then?"

"We were almost home when bang, Tommy's Chrysler careened like mad." She imitated the motion.

Bang? "Did someone shoot at you? Is that how you died?" This had been during the height of illicit liquor, and gang wars, after all. If Adriana had been murdered and the killer escaped, that would explain why she still hung around. And why she needed my assistance.

But first, she had to stop wailing. The instant I'd mentioned her death, she'd broken into sobs that would have earned her a contract with a film studio as the leading tragic girl.

"I don't mean dead, dead," I said.

She sobbed some more.

"It's true," I said, feeling like a monster. "Seeing that you're here with me."

"You're right." She calmed down. At least for now, the emotional storm had passed.

Cleo left Adriana's side and jumped onto my lap. I appreciated this sign that our new houseguest had not completely replaced me in her affection, until she hoovered up the remaining morsel of bacon on my plate.

Considering my preoccupation with food at the party last night and my authorship of the weekly blog "How To Eat Like A Queen When You're A Pauper", I could hardly blame her.

"Maybe," Adriana said. "I mean, like I said, from what I heard, Tommy's old man had been the butter and egg man for a couple of bootleggers, but Tommy was as straight as they come."

Under the table, I typed "Butter and egg man" into my search bar. Right, the man had supposedly bankrolled alcohol smugglers during the heydays of the prohibition.

If the son and heir really wanted to pull out of the business, that might explain a few things. Like being shot at.

"Was Tommy your boyfriend?"

"Geez, Louise, no. He was my sister's beau." A grin flitted over her face. "Or maybe even more. I'm not telling."

"Did the car crash?"

"Did it ever. We ended in a ditch and I went to fetch help. You walk three miles on these heels." She lifted a shapely leg to show off a strappy dance shoe.

"But you all got home safely?"

"Of course we did. I remember sneaking in through the back window and falling asleep as soon as I hit the pillow." She cast a reproachful glance in my direction, which was imitated by the cat. Those two were fast becoming bosom buddies. "That is, until someone hit me with a shoe. I'm sure I've got a bruise."

"I'm sorry," I said automatically. "Does that mean I woke you up?"

She frowned. "Maybe you didn't. I was kind of almost awake. Like, something jolted me a few minuted before. I think I heard the church bells strike eleven."

My pulse rate increased. That must have been right about when the mugger attacked me. It probably meant that in some way or another he was connected to Adriana's death. We were definitely onto something here.

Adriana draped herself against the wall. In a stomach-turning instant she sank into the wainscoting but then she was back.

I had the weird sensation she was becoming more solid. She'd always looked real and alive if a trifle pale, but that could also be attributed to her face powder. Alive, she must have turned heads everywhere.

Even dead she looked better than I ever had on my best days. She deserved at least the truth, and peace.

"What's up, Genie?" She motioned the cat towards me. "You look as if you've swallowed a frog."

"Nothing." I patted the cat, who, like Adriana, would soon be on her merry way without me and back with my mother as her rightful owner. I'd miss Cleo, but there were upsides to being without her. Eating without having to watch out for cat hair in my food was one example. "I have to go out for a bit."

"Oh, Where are we going?"

It was hard to lie to those hopeful eyes. So I settled for evasion. "Only the library. I need to do some research into our family history, to figure out which of our heirlooms will actually be useful to the museum." Including a dig into the life and times of my guest.

"The library?" She wrinkled her nose. "Isn't that all stuffy and boring? Can't we go shopping instead? Or to the park?"

"Maybe another time. And I thought I'll go alone and you keep Cleo company." I batted my eyelashes at the two.

"You can't come along."

23

"Ridiculous." Adriana pushed herself forward, only to be held back as if by invisible chains. She'd made it as far as one step from the threshold. Maybe she was somehow bound to the house.

I was already out the door but couldn't bring myself to leave her standing like this. I stepped back in, before anybody saw me talking to what presumably would be thin air to them.

Or could everybody see Adriana?

She took a deep breath as I stood beside her and moved closer to the door. "Told you I could do it."

"Wait a moment. And smile."

She made a funny face as I held up my phone camera. I could see every detail of Adriana. The camera instead registered only an empty hallway.

It also registered low battery status. A quick charge would be in order.

"Help." Adriana was pushed away from the door by an invisible force as I moved towards the living room where my charger was.

Instinctively, I rushed towards her. She promptly returned to her old spot by the door, but her pizzazz had left her. Instead, she looked bewildered.

I took a few steps back. Again, she was pushed back. I went forward and so went she.

I'd thought Adriana was bound only to the house. I was wrong. She was just as strongly attached to me, which was a problem. If I left her behind, she might lose her strength, and if we left the villa together, she also was only a shadow of her true self.

Which is why, after some trial and error, I headed towards the library with my great-great-aunt linking arms with me, and a brick I'd found in the basement weighing down my purse.

From what I gathered, that object helped because it had formed part of the house.

CHAPTER FOUR

A driana's first steps into this brave new world proved to be a howling disappointment to her. "Where are the flying cars?"

"They don't exist. We also can't fly unless in a plane or helicopter, houses do not clean themselves, more's the pity, and sickness and poverty haven't been eradicated."

She snorted in derision. "Then what have you done?"

"Invented more appliances? And set foot on the moon, more than half a century ago."

"Sheesh."

For a minute or so we both contemplated the failings of the human race before Adriana decided to make the most of what I could offer her. This included treating me to a running commentary about the neighborhood and its changes as we moved on. Still, who could blame her for pointing out the chestnut tree she'd tumbled out of as a child or the houses of boys who'd been carrying a torch for her? She skipped along the sidewalk, as carefree as a kid.

Then there were the neighborhood dogs. They all watched us stroll past. Their tails wagged and they woofed and yapped in the friendliest manner I'd ever heard them, even trained watch dogs. I had no clue if they saw Adriana or only sensed her, but whatever it was, they liked it.

A tiny bit of envy reared its ugly head. Although I was an animal lover, I'd never been welcomed by our furry neighbors in such an enthusiastic manner.

"Excuse me." A young boy whizzed past on a scooter. He evaded me, but raced right through my companion.

Yikes.

The town library, founded in 1887, occupied a gabled building at the corner of Main Street, half a block away from the museum which was its architectural twin. The round stained glass window at the top was said to be an original Tiffany design, although I doubted it.

The door swung open, wide enough for me to let Adriana through first without breaking physical contact. She probably would have been able to pass right through it though, but, as my parents had taught me, one should always mind one's manners.

The interior hadn't changed much since the 19th century. Dark wood, metal signs and the green-shaded lamps that used to be popular with banks in Adriana's era dominated the large room. One cranny was signed the children's area, and a seating area with tables allowed visitors to read or rest their feet in comfort.

"My dear Genevieve." My hero from last night beamed at me through his half-lenses. Fred sat behind the large reception desk, dressed in a natty suit and a bowtie, and leafed through a stack of books.

I gave him full marks for both his quick reaction to me entering the library, and for pronouncing my name correctly, in the French way. When it came to his attire the jury was still out.

He said, "I hope you've recovered from the shock. Have you filed a report with the police?"

"There wouldn't really have been anything to tell, would it? I mean, I didn't see the man at all, you said you didn't recognise him .and there was no damage."

He knitted his brows. "I don't like it. We pride ourselves on being such a safe, happy little community."

I gave him a reassuring smile as I scanned the name tag on his place. It read, Frederick Ward, volunteer.

Still missing from the scene was Daphne Mills, Head Librarian. "No harm done. It probably was a stranger anyway, who's by now hundreds of miles away. And we don't want to scare the good people of Cobblewood Cove unnecessarily."

He pulled out a handkerchief and cleaned his spectacles. "True, true. Now, my dear, what can I do for you?"

Since I hadn't counted on Adriana tagging along, I needed to come up with a story that would allow me to search for anything to do with her death, without upsetting her. Unobtrusively, I unlinked our arms. No change in her.

That was good. If I stayed close, my purse with the brick might be enough to anchor her in the reading nook opposite the door. There were two wide armchairs, so I might have the privacy I needed.

"I'm sorting through family stuff for the museum," I said truthfully. "So I thought, some local background would be useful. Do you have old newspapers on file? I'd like to look at 1928 to 1930." I had another idea. "And maybe some fashion magazines from that era?" One only had to see Adriana to figure out that she'd be a fan of the beauty rags.

"I'll see what I can do for you." Fred darted off, as spry as a much younger man. I warmed towards him even more, considering he'd shown no curiosity about my oddly specific request.

I steered Adriana towards the armchairs and placed the purse next to her on the floor. She twiddled her thumbs to show me how little excited she was about being here. "This place reeks of mothballs."

"It doesn't." I sniffed the air. "Well, maybe a little. They probably have to use chemicals to keep the old books intact. And don't forget, you wanted to come along."

"Excuse me? My hearing's not what it was." Fred had turned up beside us with a cart full of leather-bound volumes and a stash of Vogue.

I pointed at my earphones. "Sorry, I was talking on the phone." As excuses went, this one possessed at least a certain plausibility.

I started reading.

"Genie. Page." Adriana fluttered her eyelashes at me. I'd forgotten to count in the fact that she needed help with her magazines.

Obediently I flipped through Vogue of April 1928 until I came to a society page. That would keep her entertained for a while. I was still busy with my search for information, but until I'd pinpointed her D-Day - I'd made a mental note to avoid the word death after the earlier scene - I was going to make sure she didn't come across anything past her time that might upset her worse than the lack of flying cars.

I'd reached the end of February 1929. The Valentine's Day Massacre in Chicago had kept the local editor in a frenzy, and his reporters

CARMEN RADTKE

as well. There was speculation about a crime wave coming to all of New York State as well, and a raid on a speakeasy in town that saw a couple of Cobblewood Cove councillors, the head of the Presbyterian church board and a group of female entertainers in front of the judge's bench.

The name Darling did not feature. I wondered if my ancestors had been too cautious to get caught or too dull. I glanced at the glamorous Adriana and decided they'd probably been discerning enough to ignore the local joint with its bathtub gin and a small town band and instead preferred to live it up in the big city.

I opened the next volume. There it was, a black and white photograph of Adriana with a delicate choker necklace with a drop pendant around her neck that I itched to study up close, plus a slightly older and darker version of herself wearing a beaded headband, and two sober looking young men in spats.

I read the caption. "Annabelle and Adriana Darling with Thomas Harewood III and his cousin Richard Harewood from Vermont after the trial."

"Have a look." I showed her the page.

"That's me. And Belle." She studied every detail of the picture with laser focus. "I should have kept that short hairstyle." She twirled a finger around a curl and eyed it dubiously. "What do you think?"

"I think you'd win any beauty contest hands down."

She blew me a kiss. "You're so sweet."

"I'm honest."

She preened a little. Then she deflated. "It was really sad. Poor Tommy. His mom was such a strict teetotaler, and she barely left the house after the scandal with his daddy being in with moonshiners.

30

Such a tacky Speakeasy too." She sighed. "Next thing, his old man had a heart attack. The cousin had come to support the family during the trial, and then he stayed on. Tommy's mom went all to pieces."

"That is sad."

She ogled her picture again. "Belle is wearing your earrings."

She did, and I had overlooked it in my enthusiasm for the choker. I made Adriana return to her fashion magazine and the latest make-up trends inspired by Hollywood femme fatale Clara Bow.

I found what I'd been looking for in the October edition of the Cobblewood Cove Clarion, or Triple C as it had been affectionately known until its demise in 1998. Adriana Virginia Darling, beloved daughter, granddaughter and sister, had died at the age of 21 after a short unspecified illness.

Given that even 90-odd years after the event her complexion was glowing, this sounded suspicious. Unless ghosts could influence their appearance to look their best, she didn't look ill at all. Maybe she'd been given a fast acting poison.

"Is there a problem?" I gave a start as Fred turned up by my side. How did he do that without me noticing? "I heard you groan."

"It's fine. Just -" I lowered my voice. "Is there anyone who could tell me a bit more about personal histories?"

"You've come to the right place. My grandmother and then my mother were helping old Mrs Schuyler with the material for her society column." Now he lowered his voice. "There were a few things too hot to put in print but the notebooks are all there, in a back room."

"Could I have a peek at them?" I handed him a card with my phone number. "It would mean a lot to me."

"I don't see why not, if our librarian agrees."

31

"Thank you." He really was the nicest man I'd met in a while. I picked up my purse and signaled Adriana to rise.

"Genie! I thought it's you." Not an original greeting, but Jonathan's appreciative twinkle as he saw me step outside the library was flattering enough to relegate Fred Ward to second nicest man. "How about we continue our conversation from last night over dinner at the new French restaurant?"

"Oh." My glance darted to Adriana who nodded wildly.

"Unless I've done something to repulse you?"

"Of course not."

"I'll pick you up at eight."

Adriana whispered in my ear. "He's swell. Say yes."

I gave in. "Let's just meet there."

"Where are your glad rags?" Adriana harrumphed at the sight of my open wardrobe. I held up the blue dress from last night. It showed off my waist, without revealing too much cleavage, which made it just right for an evening in a classy restaurant.

She dismissed it with a flick of her wrist. "Too old for you." Wonderful, now she also was a fashion adviser.

I looked at the dress again. Maybe she had a point. "I have a little black dress for the exhibition opening."

"There must be something that changes you into a real dish." As if on cue, Cleo miaowed and headed for the stairs. Since I'd already planned on lugging down a few boxes from the attic, I let the two of them lead the way.

The cat pounced upon of the stacked quilts and rolled around on it. Adriana giggled. "She's just like my own little kitty."

"Maybe they're related." After all, I could see Adriana, and we were blood relatives, courtesy of her little brother Philip. Maybe the bonding thing worked the same with animals.

I climbed over boxes with old toys, a Victorian doll house and rolls of fabric and padding material for quilting until I reached the section of the attic that hopefully held the things I, or rather the Schuyler sisters, and Adriana were after.

Although everything seemed to be piled up haphazardly, the oldest trunks were stacked closest to the walls, and then everything else had accumulated over the years, according to age.

I covered a sneeze as I flung open the skylight. Dust mites danced in the air, but since I had set out reed diffusers as soon as I'd arrived, the musty smell had gone and been replaced by vanilla.

Adriana shimmied around as we reached a leather trunk. "Open it, I'm sure there's something exciting inside."

I tugged at the padlock that came with the trunk. It stayed locked. I tugged harder. Maybe I could work the clasp loose.

Adriana guffawed at my efforts. "How about using the key?"

"If I knew where it was."

She reached up to a beam and pushed. A brass key ring came in sight, only the fraction if an inch, but there could be no doubt about it. "You've touched it," I marveled.

"You're welcome."

"No, I mean, you made real contact with an object and it moved."

33

We both sat down simultaneously, open-mouthed.

"You realize what that means?" I asked.

"I might. What do you think it means?"

Honestly, I had no clue, which I admitted. Yet I would have bet my bottom dollar on what that it meant something. Well, maybe not my bottom dollar. I'd been wrong before.

The key ring held five keys, three to different trunks and two that looked like door keys.

Inside the trunk lay two silk evening dresses, carefully wrapped in tissue paper. Adriana squealed. "Aren't they spiffy? The green one is mine and the yellow one belongs to Belle." I lifted them up. The fabric still felt soft although there were a few brittle spots here and there.

My great-great-aunt narrowed her eyes as she inspected the frocks. "I'm not sure Belle's dress will fit you. You're a bit curvier, everywhere. Mom used to say it happens when you get old."

I bristled, both at the body-shaming and the dig about my age which happened to be only a decade more than that of a certain ghost.

She prattled on. "If we find a shawl, we can use safety pins to close it at the back. Can you suck in your tummy when you sit down?"

"No, and I'm not wearing this dress anyway."

She ignored me. "And there's my gloves. I wore them for my 21st birthday."

My slight pique evaporated. I pulled out the green opera gloves and stroked the soft satin. "They are fabulous."

"Do you want them?"

"They're yours." I had an idea. "How about we bring down everything that belonged to you and put it in your room?"

34

That should also keep her busy and happy while I went through the two boxes full of old documents, and had dinner with Jonathan.

"Your lipstick is on crooked. And you should wear perfume. I always do."

"It makes Cleo sneeze."

Why, oh why had I agreed to let her tag along? I already regretted my weakness as I pointed my battered Toyota towards the town hall. Everything of importance centered around the solid red brick building.

It also had parking at the back where I intended to run through rules for the evening with my companion. Again.

She continued. "Cleo's nose is too delicate for your scent because it's not French," she said. "French perfume is the best. I read that in the library."

"In a magazine from before the Great Depression."

"The what?"

The car engine sputtered.

"Let's save the history lessons for another time," I said, worrying about my Toyota, and my bank account.

Now the engine ran as smooth as silk again. Probably only an air bubble somewhere.

She fiddled with her green gloves. I had no idea how it worked, but one minute I'd held them up and the next minute they covered her slender arms up all the way over the elbows.

"That sounds boring. Like your clothes."

I decided to ignore that. The silence lasted all the way to the restaurant, and to the table in a nook where Jonathan led me and, unbeknownst to him, my spectral chaperone. Since the restaurant lacked authentic period features, the owners had opted for a mix of sleek modernism and opulence. It worked surprisingly well.

"There's no chair for me," Adriana complained as we sat down. The table next to us was free, so I moved one chair a little and placed my purse next to it.

"Allow me," Jonathan said and reached for the bag.

I moved it another inch away from him, between me and Adriana, who now lounged on the chair, singing "Yes, We have No Bananas".

I almost fell in, but I didn't want to scare away a presentable man who was paying for my dinner. As I gave him a quick check I regretted resisting Adriana's efforts to make me go out in a skirt and high heels instead of tailored slacks and ballerina flats. His suit and silk tie definitely had never seen a sales rack or a chain store.

"What would you like? They do fabulous moules marinière here, or chateaubriand if you prefer meat." He signaled the waiter.

"Beef sounds great." I mentally licked my lips.

"And red wine to go with it."

"Can I have a champagne cocktail?" a voice behind me asked.

"No." I'd answered before I could stop myself.

Jonathan gave me a puzzled look.

"To the wine. I've taken two aspirins." I touched my head and tried to appear wan. "A head bump. Serves me right for not watching where I move in the attic."

"As long as you're well enough to be out with me?"

His solicitude and eagerness to see me were touching.

"It's not that bad. I only don't mix alcohol and medication." Especially not with someone behind me who could get woozy on the fumes alone.

The pianist changed to a medley of 1960 songs while Jonathan apologized for having to go and make a business call.

"Excuse me, madam." The waiter moved Adriana's chair to offer it to an elderly lady who had come to dine with her husband. I pulled my purse closer.

"It's a bit cold and draughty here," the woman complained. "Do you have another table?"

"Draughty?" The waiter paused, as if to test the air himself. "I'm so sorry. If you will follow me."

"Serves them right for being such blisters." This time, I ignored Adriana. That is, until we were halfway through our chateaubriand and a sparkling conversation about the plans for the exhibition.

The meat went down the wrong way as Adriana hissed into my ear, "We've got to skidoo. Cleo's in danger."

CHAPTER FIVE

I coughed.

Jonathan offered me a drink of water.

Adriana gave me a pleading glance. "Please, Genie. Your beau can wait. But poor Cleo can't."

Her intensity convinced me. I took out my phone and pretended to read a message. "I'm so sorry, Jonathan. I've got to run. My mother... "

He frowned. "I thought she's not here."

"No, but I'm keeping all her emergency numbers in a folder, and she needs one of them, asap." I was halfway through the door when I remembered my manners and waved back at Jonathan who sat there with a bemused expression.

"Are you sure there's something wrong with the cat? Or did you just feel bored?" I asked as soon as we sat in the car.

She bristled. "What a mean thing to say. I can feel it in my bones."

"I believe you." I reached for her hand. For a second I really thought I could feel it before the sensation was gone.

We found the back door open and Cleo shivering under my bed. Her eyes were wild with fear and her whole body shook.

"Can you coax her out?" I asked Adriana. "We need to see if she is hurt."

I steeled myself for an emergency trip to the vet if there was so much as a scratch on Cleo. The burglars, whoever they were, must have been disturbed. My jewelry case still sat on the dresser, and my laptop was propped up on the desk.

The box with papers I'd carried down from the attic had gone. Who on earth would want to steal old photographs and diaries dating back to the 1890s?

"She's better now." Cleo snuggled against Adriana's legs, but her tail was still bushy and she seemed tense.

"Is she injured?" I knelt to stroke the soft fur. A weak miaow rewarded me.

"No, but it was a close shave. And Cleo needs a few treats. Do you have chicken breast? She thinks it might help her recover."

The tender fillet had been on tomorrow's menu but the poor kitty deserved it. We watched with relief as Cleo tore into the meat.

"I've got to call the police," I said, "but could you ask Cleo what she remembers?" As crazy as it would have sounded to me 24 hours ago, I believed that ghost and cat understood each other. Or else how could Adriana have known there were burglars in the house?

Cobblewood Cove's finest surprised me with their speed. I'd barely finished extracting information from my housemates before two officers, one male and one female, and both with the relaxed air of people used to placate elderly people, appeared on the doorstep.

They told me their names, but since Adriana cooed at Cleo, I didn't catch them properly. Instead, I nicknamed them Holmes and Marple.

The shorter of them took out her notebook while her partner checked the door for signs of entry.

"No damage, but you could pick that lock with a hairpin," he said.

Both officers fixed me with a reproachful stare.

"I'll tell my mother we need to update security."

Marple glanced around at the decor. "No kidding. You're sure something was stolen?"

"Positive. I haven't been through every room but there's at least one box missing that I'd left in the living room."

They perked up, until I told them what it contained. I could feel them giving this up as a bad case.

"There is something really wrong here," I said. "Last night I was attacked, and now my home is broken into."

"I never heard of an assault." The two officers exchanged a hopeful glance. I assumed that while a simple break-in without anything valuable stolen counted as boring, a manhunt for a violent criminal might make a nice change for them in this sleepy town.

"I fought him off, and I didn't see a face or anything." Said like that, it sounded lame.

"If you remember anything, let us know. If you want a good locksmith, my cousin runs the hardware store on Main Street. You should at least have a couple of dead-bolts." Holmes sucked his teeth. "Could have been kids alright, for a laugh."

"Do you have a lot of that?" I asked.

"Not until now we didn't."

I promised to invest in better security and to inform them if I discovered anything of value had been stolen, but they'd obviously mentally already closed the file on the case.

To be fair, I couldn't blame them. I could hardly tell them that I had reliable information from a cat that a man had prowled around the house like a hungry fox (Cleo's description, not mine, if my interpreter was to believed) and smelt so strongly of anger that she'd made a mess under the bed when his phone rang (my interpretation, confirmed by a spot of cleaning I had to do).

It would have taken a real Sherlock Holmes and Miss Jane Marple to take this case seriously.

"There should have been two," Adriana pointed out.

"There were. They always send officers in pairs, I think."

"Not the flatfoots, or is it flatfeet? The goons! He must have been casing the joint, but if he had no lookout, how was he supposed to scram if we came back?" She stroked Cleo who'd recovered enough to curl up next to Adriana.

I sneaked a glance into the mirror. It showed them together. I snapped a picture. There, we only had a cat lying on an armchair.

"Stop that," Adriana ordered. "It makes my head go all woozy."

41

"Are you okay if I go upstairs and search the attic?" I asked.

"You mean the maids' rooms? Where is the staff? Do they all have their day off together?"

"Newsflash. There is no staff anymore, unless you're rich."

"Oh." A long drawn pause, which surprised me. So far, Adriana had taken everything she'd experienced about the 21st century in her stride, but then she'd already grown up with telephones, automobiles and most appliances. The only thing that had gone the way of the dodo were the maids and footmen.

An ugly thought raised its head. "Are there more of you in this house?"

She blinked at me in confusion.

"Ghosts. Are there more departed souls hanging around?" I'd discounted family, but what if there was a servant with a justified grudge? If my book and movie knowledge were correct, having decent employers was a lottery, and even good guys would have thought it their right to get handsy with a pretty maid.

"I haven't seen anyone."

"Good. But you'll tell me if anyone pops up?"

She saluted me. "Aye, aye, Captain."

I was halfway up the stairs when the doorbell rang.

Adriana and I collided as I ran down. Or at least we would have collided if she hadn't distorted herself to make way for me. And if she'd still had a real body.

With every hour I found it harder to remember she was a specter.

Outside the door stood Jonathan. "Are you okay?" he asked without preamble. "I saw a police car outside your door."

"He's sweet on you," Adriana whispered. "I bet he's been pacing up and down the street just to gather his nerve."

"It was nothing. Just kids who probably picked the locks because of a dare. I shouldn't even have called the police on that." My laughter rang hollow in my ears.

"You're not a bad liar." My housemate couldn't resist the temptation to join the conversation.

"That's awful. Did they cause any damage?" His blue eyes shone with concern. "I could send a handyman to help you."

"Seriously, there's no need. Everything is fine and tomorrow I'll have a stronger lock installed." I remembered my manners. "Would you care to come inside for a coffee or something stronger?"

He seemed torn. "Rain check? I'm sure you could do with some rest."

Adriana heaved a dramatic sigh as I closed the door. "He reminds me of Tommy's cousin. The same built and that smile..." She waltzed a few steps around me. "He should take us dancing the next time he asks us out. What do you say, Cleo?"

The cat, who'd prudently stayed on top of the staircase seemed to give the feline equivalent of a shrug and headed for the bedroom.

The coffee machine which had been my one contribution to the kitchen equipment, beeped. I reached for the frother. A thick layer of milk foam on top of my usual strong French roast would help me sort my thoughts. I looked around. The kitchen was suspiciously empty.

Where was everyone? Normally, Cleo demanded her breakfast loud and clear if I so much as moved under the duvet. Today though, the silence was thick enough to set my heart racing.

Suppose Cleo hadn't been alright. She could have suffered a heart attack. After all, she was a mature cat. At least it said on the cat food I'd been handed for her that it was for senior cats.

I put the frother down. "Cleo? Adriana?"

"Don't shout." Adriana glided into the room, followed by her adoring sidekick. "I was only fixing my hair."

To me it looked exactly the same as before, with not a single strand out of place, just like her make-up was perfect. I bit my tongue. If I had learned one thing since this whole business had started, it was that Miss Adriana Darling took beauty seriously, hers and mine.

She eyed my messy ponytail. "We need to do something about you."

"All I need is coffee." I reached for the milk container. "And maybe a few ideas about what's going on."

She sat down, demurely. "I'll have toast with my coffee, please. And lightly scrambled eggs."

At least we had the same taste in breakfast. And she said thank you.

While I ate and Adriana enjoyed the idea of having food, I called the number of the hardware store the police officer had written down before he left. To be on the safe side, I asked the sales assistant of the aptly named "Nuts and Bolts" to send someone around with a complete assortment of safety locks and window bolts.

I didn't truly expect another break-in, because, let's face it, by now the whole town would have heard about police and the Darling villa and would be on the look-out. Neighborhood watch was alive and well in these places.

As was customer service. I'd just finished the dishes and put a new dishwasher on my growing list of things needed to bring the house into the 21st century, when a lanky guy in coveralls stood outside the door. Cleo had fled at the ring of the bell.

"That was fast," I said.

"I brought the new locks," he said. A sewn-on name tag told me I was dealing with Bert, who seemed to be the taciturn type. "Back door, right?" He held up a tool box with nicotine stained fingers.

"And the front door and the garage and the windows."

He gaped. "Mr Jonathan didn't say that."

Now it was my turn to stare. "You're not from the hardware store?" I maneuvered him back out. "I'm afraid it's a misunderstanding."

"But Mr Jonathan--"

"Has been very kind but I've got everything under control."

He had no choice but to retreat.

News must have been airborne in Cobblewood Cove. The person I'd hired, a cheerful red-head called Jolene Ortega, was still working on the second-floor windows, when Matt paid me a visit.

"Don't tell me," I said. "You saw a police car last night."

"No, Dahlia and Primrose sent me to check on your wellbeing."

"Gosh darn," Jolene shouted. "Do you have a band aid? I don't want to drip on your carpet. Blood's a bummer to get out."

"Coming." Blood sounded ominous.

"I'll come along if you don't mind," he said. "I've done enough first aid courses to qualify as a volunteer paramedic."

We found Jolene holding up her thumb. She'd swaddled it in a now reddish strip of fabric.

I winced. I'm squeamish when it come to bodily fluids.

"May I?" Matt took her hand and gently unwrapped the finger. A nasty gash ran halfway down the first digit. "Do you have current tetanus?"

She nodded. "And rabies shots, and tick shots, whatever doc says I should have."

"How did you hurt yourself?" I asked. The window frame and sill looked perfectly harmless to me.

She pointed at a bloody razor blade. "That part where the window locks? That was hidden right under it, to stop the lock from catching properly. Either somebody had used it to try and break in and forgotten, or you're dealing with kids who have a sick idea of pranks."

"They'd also need to have uncanny climbing skills." The windows were high, and although an apple tree stood right outside, its top branches barely took the weight of a cat.

Jolene closed her eyes.

"I'll take you to a doctor," Matt said. "You'll need stitches."

"I'll come right back and finish the job," she promised me as she lagged down the stairs.

"Only if you're well enough, okay?"

"I'll make sure the lady follows doctor's orders," Matt reassured me.

Adriana waited until the door was locked behind them until she made an appearance. "I don't like these things," she said.

I agreed. I had to figure out what on earth was going on. That Adriana was the key, seemed obvious to me. And that this house held an important secret about her death and possibly her murderer.

As crazy as it sounded, even after all these generations, whatever it was must pose a threat to someone.

CHAPTER SIX

G oing out on my own gave me a weird sensation. Nobody who whispered in my ear, no brick to carry around, and no making sure that I kept to my role and never spoke to a, to all accounts invisible, person in public.

Adriana had been anything but pleased to stay behind, until I reminded her of the possible dangers to poor Cleo, were the cat left all alone.

Cleo apparently had agreed. I forbore to mention that a ghost was hardly a match for a burglar or worse, but since I didn't expect any attempt to break in broad daylight, they should be happy enough.

It also helped that I remembered Lottie's movie collection. She'd been an avid Buster Keaton and Charlie Chaplin fan. Several "Tramp" and "General"-themed pillowcases were ample proof. They dated back to an earlier crafting era, before tapestries and quilts took over. I'd selected the longest running dvd, switched it on and left Adriana to watch.

Fred Ward dealt with another reader as I entered the library, carrying gifts.

I'd had the foresight of stopping at the Cocoa Cabana on my way. Tiny, individually wrapped artisanal truffles that could be enjoyed in one bite, and macaroons in all colors of the rainbow would hopefully pave my way with the head librarian, if the cookie tin and the crumbs behind her desk that I'd spotted yesterday belonged to her.

Fred stamped two books and sent the customer on her way. It cheered me no end that things here were still done the old-fashioned way. People who meant business when it came to history tended to be fountains of knowledge about everything. Which also meant that Fred already was aware of the break-in and that I'd hired Jolene.

"I've got window bars at the back and a doorbell camera," he told me as we sat down for a chat.

"That is impressive," I said. "The police told me nothing ever happened in this town and that it must have been bored kids."

He snorted. "Ridiculous. Our teenagers might get up to a bit of no good, but please, my dear, what should they want in your house? There's no money or no trophy like the one in high school cabinet that's been pinched twice by neighboring teens until the school board decided on safety glass."

I unwrapped a truffle. We'd put them in a bonbon dish in the small kitchen, except for a handful for personal use.

"I found a death notice in the archived newspaper yesterday," I said. "Adriana Darling. It didn't say exactly what she died of, only that she was very young."

He adjusted his spectacles. "Let me think." I let the hazelnut truffle melt in my mouth as he pondered my question. "I won't be two

49

moments." He hurried off, with a spring in his step. I smiled to myself. I'd found the right person to help me.

He returned with a wrapped scrapbook and two pairs of gloves. "I'm afraid you'll have to wear these. The paper is old, you see, and we don't want it to deteriorate." He donned a pair of gloves himself and took the scrapbook out of its plastic sleeve.

I opened it with the required reverence.

"It belonged to one of your ancestors," he said in an apologetic tone, "but it was left to the library."

"That's strange. There are tons of family papers in the attic. Do you have more Darling tomes?"

"This is the only one that I'm aware of." An impish smile flitted over his round face. "Of course there's also the notebooks I told you about. I'm happy to make an appointment with you to view them in our back room."

"That's great." I beamed at him. What a pity my mother already had a husband. Otherwise I'd have set her up with Fred.

The scrapbook held mostly party invitations for Adriana and Annabelle to debutante balls, Christmas parties and sleigh rides. Interspersed were photographs showing Adriana and her sister growing up from wide-eyed babies to young girls in starched clothes, with a sparkle to them that the camera had caught perfectly.

I thought about my great-great-aunt who was hopefully laughing herself silly right now over Laurel and Hardy.

It really wasn't fair that she had to die so young.

"Can I take a few pictures?" I asked. There should have been lots of old photos up in the attic, but if this all was about Adriana, I wouldn't bet that the albums from her era were still there.

"By all means."

I snapped away and then put the cell phone aside. I'd come to the important bit. In an expressive copperplate, the owner of the scrapbook had written, "A catastrophe has befallen us. Dr Bowen had to be called in the middle of the night, for Adriana has come down with a raging fever after being forced to a nightly walk over icy roads."

That must have been the path she'd told me about, after Tommy's car had burst a tyre and they'd ended in the ditch.

I read on. "Thanks to her selfless undertaking, her beloved sister has suffered no adverse effects to her health, but our hearts are heavy when we see Adriana lying in her room, drifting in and out of consciousness."

The doctor had diagnosed double pneumonia. Apparently, Adriana had been drenched from head to toe when she slipped off the roadside and into an icy stream. She'd have drowned, if not for a tree and a strong branch which allowed her to climb out.

Five days after the doctor first came to see her, she took her last breath, and the scrapbook ended.

"Of course," I said to myself.

"Pardon?" Fred blinked at me.

"I was wondering why the scrapbook was left to you. It must have been too painful to bear, having it in the house."

For now I knew at least what had happened to Adriana all those decades ago. So, okay, nobody could have foreseen she'd die of pneumonia, but what was obvious to me was that the burst tyre was no accident.

Anyone who had any clue about Adriana could also count upon her making sure her sister was safe and looked after by the boyfriend while she went for help.

That tumble into the stream? I remembered the man who'd attacked me, and the shove that went with it. I was sure Adriana had been pushed.

Whoever was behind this had intended her to drown. While she had saved herself that fateful night, he'd succeeded after all.

Adriana Darling had been murdered, and she'd come back to help me unmask the culprit once and for all.

CHAPTER SEVEN

"**G**enie?" Fred appeared concerned.

I snapped out of my musings and gave him a winsome smile. "I wonder if you could do me a favor, or rather, my mother."

"Sure." The mere mention of Aimée brought a twinkle to his eyes.

"If you could make copies of everything to do with Adriana and Belle Darling? Mother is so interested in family history, and that whole era in particular." I pointed at my Art Deco inspired earrings. "She sparked my career with her enthusiasm."

Mentally, I crossed my fingers behind my back. Aimée had many hobbies. Digging up the past did not feature among them.

He adjusted his spectacles. "I wonder ..."

"Any form would be fine," I said. "Photocopies, screenshots, whatever is available and won't damage the originals."

"We might have the *Clarion* on microfiche," he said. "That technology is a little before your time, I assume, but back then Cobblewood Cove was cutting edge."

"You're a star," I said. "I'l pop in tomorrow and pick the copies up." With a little wave, I dashed off.

Adriana sputtered with indignation. "Somebody popped me? I ended up with a Chicago overcoat?"

"Not exactly. They didn't shoot you, but I'm afraid they meant you to die."

I'd practiced my words all the way home, but Adriana was made of sterner stuff than I'd feared. Well, at least mentally she was.

The more hours I spent with her, the more often I found myself reaching out to touch her for comfort. If she was this vibrant and real in her afterlife, she must have been irresistible while technically alive.

She stomped around now, judging by her movements. If I listened closely, I could imagine hearing her heels klick on the wooden floor in the living room.

"Those goons won't get away with it. We'll nail them and send them to the slammer."

"That's the spirit. We can at least name and shame them even if they've been dead and buried for ages. But what's even more important, once we've solved your case, we'll also solve all the rest."

She gave an excited little squeal. "We'll be gumshoes."

I affected a deep drawl and pulled an imaginary hat into my face. "Partner, we're about to blow this case wide open."

"Where do we start?"

I had just opened my mouth to answer, when the door bell rang. I'd been in town for almost a week, with only the Schuylers reaching out to me, and suddenly I was more popular than a prom queen with a brand new dance card.

"Told you I'd be back," Matt said.

"Ask him inside," Adriana said.

I obliged.

"He's a sheikh," she declared after circling him. "The other one was swell, but this one is the spit image of Valentino. I cried my eyes out when he died." Her eyes became misty.

"How's Jolene?" I asked our visitor.

"Couple stitches. She plans on coming over later, when the meds have worn off." He narrowed his eyes. There really was a resemblance to the brooding good looks of Hollywood's original latin lover. "Whoever did that might come back."

"But there's nothing to steal here, unless they're quilt aficionados, and even then they could simply ask if they could buy them."

"Maybe there is something valuable in these rooms and you're unaware of it."

Yes, I thought, like some tangible proof someone is desperate to recover. But who'd care after all these years? Most families had a skeleton or two in the closet.

To go to these lengths to cover up an ancestor's wrongdoings, a man had to stand to lose something very important to him. In a town like Cobblewood Cove, that meant his business or his social standing. Usually those two were intertwined. I filed away that thought.

"Do you mind if I have a look around?"

Adriana batted her eyelashes at him..

"If you think that helps?" I didn't want to shoo him out, but the timing could have been better. I needed a good heart-to-heart with my fellow gumshoe. Matt was a third wheel.

"It might." He cast his experienced eye over the wall tapestries. "There are a number of masterpieces hanging around that the owner bought in a thrift shop."

"Or looted paintings brought back as war souvenirs." I'd read the stories. "Somehow I still don't think that you'll find treasures in this house. If there was something, it'll be long gone. The house sat empty for weeks between Lottie's death and my arrival."

Nevertheless, I followed Matt from room to room, while Adriana ogled him more and more shamelessly. Good on her, I thought amused.

"Nothing that pops out," he declared when we ended the tour. "Although those vintage dresses and jewelry do well at auctions, especially when they're as beautiful and well preserved as yours."

"Why, thank you." Adriana twirled. The silky fabric clung to her curves exactly where it was supposed to cling. "I've been told I have the best taste in the whole county."

"If you want to sell them, I could arrange that."

"What?" Adriana gave him an angry poke. "Those are mine."

He frowned.

"Is anything wrong?" I asked.

"It's nothing. Just a trifle warm."

Adriana and I shared an astonished look behind his back. So far I'd been the only one not feeling any kind of cold or draught when my great-great-aunt was near. On Matt, she had the opposite effect.

He opened Jolene's tool box which she'd left behind. "If you don't mind, I'll install the lock. That'd give Jolene the chance to take it easy for a little longer."

"Shouldn't we make sure there are no other dangerous surprises?" I poked the wooden frame with a chisel. Matt took the tool away from me and grabbed a torch.

"There's nothing," he declared after shining the light on every inch of wall and window.

He worked fast and with precision while I watched. Not that I feared he would botch the job or that I thought he'd abscond with the second key to the window lock or copy it, but I'd decided not to trust anyone at this stage. Also, Matt had been one of the few people who knew when I was leaving the Schuyler's party, and that I'd be walking home.

Watching Matt also gave me the chance to keep an eye on Adriana. She seemed to enjoy herself with a personable man around, but I didn't want her feelings to get hurt. All it would take was one unflattering comment on something close to her heart. That could easily be the tacky still-life of a flower vase that was hanging in the hallway instead of gracing a bonfire, where it belonged.

It had been painted by a Darling bride around when Adriana was born.

If Matt thought himself alone, he might be tempted to say something. I would, in his stead. Indeed I had thought a few choice words and none of them bore repeating in public.

I made another mental note to gauge how Adriana felt about the painting. In the meantime, I could offer it to the museum as a loan. Or a permanent donation, as an example about the pastime of Cobblewood Cove's upper crust before the Great War.

"All done." He stepped back to admire his handiwork.

"Thank you," I said. "Would you like something to drink?"

"Coffee would be good."

He had the knack of fitting in, I realized as we sat in the kitchen. There were no awkward pauses or signs of ego as we chatted about traveling.

Most men acted as if they had something to prove when I mentioned that I'd grown up all over the world.

I had gotten used to stories about frequent flier miles, the best little restaurants in the worlds greatest cities (most of them tourist traps straight out of airline magazines, as one of them had told me in a moment of honesty), and other kind of verbal strutting.

Instead, Matt said, "That must have been liberating but also lonely at times."

"It was, once in a while." Saying goodbye to yet another bunch of friends and another place I'd grown used to, and start all over again in a new school had been fun when I was little, but not so much as I grew up.

At least my parents had enrolled me in English-speaking schools wherever we went. I could get by in a few languages, but I'd never been expected to tackle exams in a foreign tongue. "But I always had our dog and Aimée."

He raised his eyebrows. "My mother. Or mom, mum, maman, Mami and whatever the equivalent was. It got confusing so I used her first name instead." I grinned. "When she married my dad, she'd been plain Amy, but as a devoted Francophile she switched the spelling. It suits her."

It did. Even in her 50s, Aimée oozed effortless style, and she never went without a silk scarf knotted around her throat just so.

"Is that why she named you Geneviève? She was the patron saint of Paris, wasn't she?" He pronounced my name the French way.

Aimée would have been won over in an instant. So was Adriana. She had implored me to place Matt next to her, and while he and I chatted, she discreetly touched his hand.

I averted my gaze. I should have put a stop to it, but on the other hand, he didn't know and she deserved a little harmless flirtation.

"Are you planning any changes to the house?" Matt asked. "It's such a classic design for the area. I've convinced the Schuyler sisters to include a side exhibition on the architect in the museum."

"I have no idea who designed the villa," I said. "But it's up to Aimée what she intends to do, with Lottie gone."

"Is she returning here soon?"

Little hairs on my neck rose. Why was he asking? And why would he have any idea who had been the original architect?

I plastered a smile on my face. "She likes to be spontaneous."

Luckily, her new husband shared Aimée's sense of adventure. As the co-owner of a successful company, Tony had the good fortune to only work when he was needed, and to be able to do video conferences. At 60 he was too young and active to do nothing.

"What about you? Where is your home?" That was a question to which I'd have liked to have the answer myself, but now was neither the time nor place for it. Especially since Adriana had no idea that Cleo's doting owner would return soon and that she'd have to say good-bye to the cat, and to me, unless she'd already passed over to the other side by then.

Instead, I pretended to check my phone. "Drat," I said. "I'm afraid I've got to go. Can't neglect everything."

"That's alright." He flashed his gleaming teeth at me. It almost came as a relief to see that he had slightly crooked molars. They added to the character in his face. Without furrowed brows and unconscious smoldering, he bore little resemblance with Valentino, apart from the dark hair and eyes.

"He'll be back," Adriana prophesied when we were finally alone. "Did you see those shoulders?"

"I'd feel better if we could count him out," I said.

She made a face. "So, what's our next move, partner, if we want to clear our new beau?"

"I'm going to the town hall. I dimly remember them having a portrait gallery of sorts, with all the movers and shakers," I said. "If I have any idea who were the big cheeses a century ago and which of those families still hold sway, that might lead us somewhere."

"If you take me along, I can tell you everything about them." She hopped up on the table and dangled her legs. "Believe me, some of these stories will blow off your socks." She batted her lashes at me. "I might remember a lot more if we could go to the pictures again?"

I must have looked blank, because she said, "In the drawing room? With your private screen?"

I rifled through the movie collection. I needed something that wasn't too far removed from Adriana's era, but maybe with a little more plot, and not silent. Otherwise, I'd have to resort to streaming, and a little shopping for classic movies.

We were in luck. Adriana's eyes grew rounder and rounder as I treated her to her first acquaintance with "What Happened One Night" and the fabulous Claudette Colbert.

She giggled and oohed in all the right places, until we came to the scene when Clark Gable takes off his shirt. The tv and DVD player both froze and unfroze, the lights crackled and flickered.

Cleo jumped out of her basket and stood there, her tail bushing and fur sticking up.

I hit the pause button. The lights behaved normal again but I switched them off. The wiring in the house was old, and overload was always a risk.

Adriana pouted. "The reel is broken."

I hit play. "It's modern technology. We can stop a movie whenever we want to."

Cleo calmed down and returned to her spot, while I wondered about my game plan.

Since I felt uncomfortable leaving Adriana and Cleo alone until I'd spoken to an electrician, I opted for an overdue visit to the pet massage salon Cleo's owner swore by for my feline charge, while my partner-in-crime and I went to look at mediocre paintings.

"She says we should stay and be pampered too," Adriana said. "She says your fur will come out in clumps if you don't relax more."

"Cleo appears to say a lot."

"We're friends. We talk. And she's right."

"Isn't it amazing how you both tend to agree?"

Adriana allowed herself a self-satisfied grin. "People like to spill the beans to me. I guess it works on cats as well. And a massage and manicure would be nice."

She gave my short, unvarnished fingernails a pointed stare.

Her own were almond shaped and perfectly groomed but also left natural.

It dawned on me what she was angling for. "You want a girl's night in. Chatting, and painting each other nails."

"And a mimosa?"

I nodded. Maybe the fact that you'd been killed and were trying to uncover who and why didn't disturb your cheerfulness overmuch when you were dead.

It did disturb me though.

CHAPTER EIGHT

I eyed Fred with a new detachment.

He'd been so generous with his support, right from the start. And he'd been on the spot when I needed help. But what if that had been the plan all along? Was that why he denied being able to identify the mugger although he'd seen the whole incident?

I'd certainly trusted him, as an old admirer of my mother's, and turned to him as a reliable source. While he had no idea why I was so interested in certain years and events, he was the one who fed me that information.

He was also the one who could tell exactly what I had seen or read. Add to that his chumminess with my main suspects and he topped my list of probable spies.

"More tea?" I refilled his cup with darjeeling without waiting for his answer. He could have sat model for inoffensive pensioner of the year, with his rosy cheeks and old-fashioned suspenders. To think I'd fallen for his helpful little act.

He stirred in sugar. "Mind if I dunk?", he asked as I offered him ginger snaps from Butler's Pantry. I'd been told they were his favorite. "It's my upper plate that's giving me trouble."

"Don't think about it." Were we both trying to put each other at ease, I with my perfect hostess act and he with his confession about his dental state?

He soaked the ginger nut in the tea and nibbled with all signs of enjoyment. His munching sounded exactly like Cleo.

Adriana, who had circled him like a hungry shark for a while, because his aftershave reminded her of her dad, now rested on the couch.

"Have the Schuylers always been the leading lights of Cobblewood Cove?" I asked. "I'd have thought that your family, with its long history, could easily rival them."

He twinkled at me. "That's very astute of you and very kind. But those of us who don't search the limelight can also do our duty. If you ask me, all that really matters is honor, and doing the right thing. One doesn't have to be top of the tree for that."

"I wouldn't say producing several mayors is something to ignore. You're hiding your light under a bushel, Fred."

He sat a little straighter. Flattery will do that to a man, and to many women too.

I piled it on. "Just take that newspaper clipping you showed me this morning. Re-elected for the third time. Don't tell me the Mayor Ward of the 1920s wasn't every bit as important as Steward Schuyler, blue-blooded bride or not."

He dunked another ginger nut. "Old Horace liked to stay out of the limelight and steer the city's fate from behind the scenes. All Wards do. And, to be honest, the Schuylers have the looks to be plastered all over the news. I'm more than happy to leave that to the current head of the house. I've done my bit in the council, with close on 30 years of service, and now I enjoy my retirement, the library, and growing roses."

He nodded at the enormous bouquet of pink double blossomed glowers he'd presented me with. "My Queen Elizabeth is famous all over the county. Three years running as gold medalist at the flower show." He straightened a stem. "No chance of that if I were to do my duty at the council."

"So, who is running the show? I thought the Schuyler sisters were the last family members around."

"You haven't meet the nephew yet? I believe he was out of town on urgent business. Smart man, very smart. Good with money too. He doubled the family fortune just like that on the stock market, and pulled out the investment before things got shaky. He's doing big deals with Japan too, I believe." Adriana's mouth formed an o. Inwardly, I had the same reaction. "That's impressive."

"Having a Duchess in the family tree helped the Schuyler a lot over the years. They'd kill to keep to that way, as the saying goes. Mind you, I don't see what's wrong with pulling yourself up by the bootstraps, but that's between us."

I mimed zipping my lips. Adriana copied me. She hated being left out of a conversation for too long.

Fred gave me a grateful smile. "Have you found anything of interest in the notebooks?"

"A few tidbits. I never knew we had a speakeasy in town, and a raid. How exciting."

"Ah, right. Now that's a bit of a sore spot." He rubbed his nose.

"But there's nothing to be ashamed about, is there? I mean, what's the Roaring Twenties without a bit of boozing and wild parties?" If my carefree laughter appeared a little rehearsed, that's because it was. Adriana had taught me.

I caught her glance and satisfied nod.

Fred's spectacles steamed up a little, and not from the tea. Something made him uncomfortable about the subject.

"Don't tell me you had gangsters in town. Cobblewood Cove as a mob hotbed?"

"Gosh, no." He squirmed a little. "But there were a few unsavory incidents."

I leant closer. "Like what?"

The pink in his rosy cheeks deepened. "Some folks who should've been in the poorhouse were suddenly flush, and a certain boarding-house outside the city limits on the clifftop had more visitors than it should've had."

"Booze and beauties?"

"Nothing was ever proven, but there was a lot of unease. A lot, especially with all those turf wars in Chicago."

"And we're not too far from the border, or main routes to the lakes." If someone in town was actually in bed with Al Capone or his rivals, now that'd be a cause for scandal even today. Especially if your wealth had a lot to do with the pristine reputation of your family.

I had one last question. "Whatever happened after the raid?"

He goggled. "Honestly, my dear Genie, I have no idea."

"Doesn't matter. Have another cookie."

When he toddled off, I had a lot to mull. While I had no intention to scratch Fred off my list of suspects just yet, he'd given me another man who deserved some scrutiny. A visit to the Schuyler sisters and a nice long chat were overdue. But first I needed to select some items to take along.

"What a funny little man," Adriana said as we made our way to the attic.

"Fred? I thought you liked him." I pulled out an old trunk and dusted off the slight film that had built up since I'd first arrived and given everything a quick wipe.

"I do," she said. "But geez, what an old stick in the mud he became, just because you asked about the old gin mills and a few molls."

I flung open the lid. "It might not have been a big deal to you, but I'm sure the elders would have more than frowned upon anyone who did more than have a drink or two and a quick dance. If you were the man behind it, what would that mean?"

Pearly laughter rang in my ears. "Those stiffs? Not a fat chance. Or else why would old Schuyler have to pay off the mayor to get out of a jam?"

She reached for the fringed silk shawl I'd taken out. "That's mine. Isn't it spiffy? I love that bronze color."

My mind reeled. "Mayor Ward took bribes?" How did that fit with Fred's high opinion about the honor of his family? If that particular little piece of information became public, he could say goodbye to the Ward's good reputation.

"At least that's what Daddy said. He told Belle to stay away from trouble, because he'd hate to see his daughters in the cooler or have to crawl to the mayor with dough in his hand."

Her eyes were still on the shawl. If she could slip into her gloves, maybe she could wear this too. The hairs on my neck stayed put as she draped it loosely around her shoulders. It shouldn't have worked but it did. She swayed a little, and the long shawl fringe moved with her - all while still being physically in my hands.

I took a couple of deep, grounding breaths. This whole new world took some adjustment.

We discovered a few pieces that had belonged to an aunt that had lived with Adriana's family. Bustled skirts, high-necked blouses and Victorian jet bracelets imported from the English seaside town of Whitby would be the right kind of contributions to the museum. Adriana had hardly given them a second glance and declared them too dreary for words.

We'd also found more of her things, including a hand-painted blue and silver kimono I wouldn't have minded owning myself. I'd hoped to stumble upon the choker Adriana had worn on the photograph as well, but hadn't so far.

I smoothed a blouse. Everything had been so well wrapped and protected from moths, the colors were still vivid.

The Schuyler sisters should be happy, I decided. And if they were guilty of deception, two, or rather three could play that game.

CHAPTER NINE

F red waited for me with copies of newspaper articles. Adriana peered over my shoulder as my new friend put down one item after another in front of me. It would have felt churlish to grab the lot and run, so I decided to stay a little, despite Adriana's signals to the contrary.

The columns from the Triple C were full of gossip and gushing descriptions of fashion and of major events.

The odd photograph or two added to the intrigue when the caption would only name the gentleman, a tanned guy in a pinstriped suit and a white Panama hat, but not the woman by his side.

In every picture her face was obscured by a veiled hat, but the hems of her dresses were short enough to draw everyone's eyes without causing outright scandal. Her high heels brought her up to his ear and in one photograph she snuggled close enough to him that it'd be difficult to put so much as a sheet of paper between them. "Mr Steward Schuyler and friend," I read aloud.

"Do you have any idea who that woman is?" I asked. Adriana took another peek, as did Fred. Their heads were so close together they almost touched.

"Not the future Mrs Schuyler, that much is sure," Fred said. "He went up in the world and married an aristocrat."

I whistled through my teeth.

"It happened a lot," Fred said. "Us Americans had the money, and the Europeans had the titles and family trees and not a dime in their pockets. It was the war that did it."

"Did Mr Schuyler go on a fashionable grand tour to the old world to meet a bride?"

Fred guffawed. "No, the Schuylers always stuck close to home. Still do. He would have been afraid that someone else would swoop in and become the new king of Cobblewood Cove if he so much as left the East coast. He met his good lady in Boston."

He searched through another book of clippings until he landed on a page solely devoted to wedding photographs. They were dated a week or so before Adriana set out on her fateful trip.

Next to Stewart Schuyler stood a dark-haired young woman, clad in silk and furs. A small hat perched on her marcelled hair, and pearls and diamonds glittered on her ears and neck.

"Duchess Tatiana, that's who she was. Her family fled the Bolsheviks, and she arrived here with next to nothing." Fred blew his nose, deeply affected by his story.

"I know London and Paris were teeming with Russian refugees," I said, admiring the jewelry. My best guess was Cartier. "Most of them had a fortune in family jewels hidden away, but I assume his Duchess wasn't one of them. She kept her expensive taste though. This is the among the best American money would buy."

"I don't think Stewart would have wanted it any other way. The family had a reputation to upkeep, after all, and the Schuylers take those things real serious."

Adriana giggled. "I bet they do. This is too, too good." She knew something I didn't then.

Fred presented two more clippings to me.

One showed a group of young women returning from their year at a finishing school in Switzerland, and the other was dedicated to the fine swearing-in ceremony and subsequent ball for Cobblewood Cove's mayor Horace Ward, who'd been re-elected in a landslide for the third time.

He had a sly expression, and I could easily imagine him accepting money for favours rendered. His wife, a good-natured, plump woman dressed in sensible blouse and costume, cut a cake. She wore a triple-strand pearl necklace which might or might not have been the real thing.

There couldn't have been a bigger contrast to the new Mrs Schuyler.

"Your ancestor?" I asked.

"Seven mayors in the Ward family since Teddy Roosevelt's days." He smoothed back a fly-away strand of hair. "And not a single scandal among them."

I stifled a smirk.

Adriana eyeballed the photo. "There's something I heard. I think. Or - oh, my head's all spinning."

Fred gave me a wink. "Well, there might be some juicier bits in the things they didn't print." He tapped his fingers on the notebooks.

"Could I borrow them?"

My question took him aback. "Take them out of the library?"

"I promise I'll protect them with my life. I just don't feel as if I should leave the villa unguarded for too long." I gave him a brave little smile. "After what happened."

"That's true. I hope you haven't had yet another scare. Some would have long since ran a mile."

"I promised to help out with material for the museum and I intend to stick to my word."

"Spoken like a true Darling." He slid the notebooks over to me.

"Did we ever hold a position of power in this town?" I asked, in case he wondered about my interest in the other old families.

"Not power as such, no. The Darlings tended to be more about culture and bold new ideas, not so much about holding office."

"Daddy sat on three boards even though they were the most crashing bores," Adriana protested. "And Mommy volunteered at the Red Cross and she hosted the suffragettes for coffee and committees."

"You're very generous, Fred," I told him as I picked up the notebooks. Again, my hands were gloved but this time I'd come prepared and brought my own.

"When will you be finished with them? I could come over tonight or tomorrow."

"Tomorrow would be fine. After dinner? Or maybe for afternoon tea?" This British invention had been a staple of Aimée's, both for the food and for the cultured impression it made. It also had the effect of loosing tongues if their owners were plied with assorted sweets and gallons of tea or coffee.

It worked like a charm. We agreed on an hour, and I left with the notebooks carefully wrapped and put in a box.

I congratulated myself that I'd brought a large folder along as well, so I could safely store them in my purse before I bode my helpful new friend a fond farewell. At long last, Adriana and I were on our merry way.

The town hall stood on the other side of the square.

From the front, one saw an impressive brick building with a large frieze showing plant motifs under the cornice. At the back, where dumpsters lined a service alley, the largesse had stopped and not a single decorative element had increased the expenditure.

I wondered who had been responsible for that decision.

Inside, the same duality existed. My steps echoed on intricate parquet flooring reminiscent of European palaces and banisters and balustrades leading up the staircase were carved by a master's hand and polished within an inch of their life.

Behind the office doors, things changed. I'd been there a few times and remembered squeaking floorboards straight from the sawmill, hard chairs and metal filing cabinets.

Today, we stuck to the hallway where Cobblewood Cove's finest hung in all their oil painted glory.

As expected, the Schuylers jostled for pride of place with the Harewoods.

Adriana pulled a disgusted grimace as she came face to face with the portrait of Tommy's dad.

To me, old Harewood looked disappointingly ordinary for the local equivalent of a member of the mob. His fur coat and diamond tie pin left little doubt as to his status, but apart from that, he looked no different from the other honoraries around the turn of the last century.

What did surprise me instead was finding several Wards in the gallery. Sadly, no more portraits had been added after World War II, so I couldn't be sure how much had changed when it came to ruling the local roost.

What I could tell was that the old pecking order had been made of the Schuylers, the Harewoods and the Wards. Not a single Darling greeted me from inside the gilded frames, but my family's name was displayed prominently on a plaque commemorating donors and sponsors.

Ariana hummed to herself all the way home, lost in sweet memories.

I would have to introduce her to some more modern music. The 1920s tunes had their appeal, but there was a limit to how often I could listen to "If You Knew Susie Like I knew Susie" and "Yes Sir, That's My Baby" without having it stuck in my ear and brain permanently.

Adriana insisted on a cappuccino to jog her memory as we settled down with our reading material.

I took out the milk frother and whipped up the milk while she perched on the sofa, smiling sweetly.

I switched to decaf to be on the safe side. If one whiff of brandy went to her head, I didn't want to risk an overload of caffeine.

I sipped, my great-great-aunt sniffed, and Cleo purred while we went through the copies again.

As kind and easy-going as Fred was, a coffee stain on precious historical documents might prove to be too much to bear even for him, so I'd decided to wait with the notebooks until my irrepressible companion had finished inhaling our cappuccino.

A rosy fingertip hovered over the milk foam.

"Stop that," I said.

Her face fell. "I've never had this new kind, ever, in my whole life." A dramatic little wobble accompanied her words, supposed to tug on my heartstrings.

It worked. I scooped a spoonful of milk foam out and put it on a saucer.

Cleo's tongue shot out in perfect synchronicity with Adriana's finger. They both licked their lips in unison, too. Soulmates, I thought amused.

"Show me that last page again," Adriana said after the milk foam had vanished and Cleo licked her whiskers clean.

She scrutinized Stewart Schuyler and his veiled lady friend, and then the wedding shots back and forth. It took her so long, I had the urge to go and do something else instead of swiping back and forth on the screen.

"Ha." She jumped to her feet. "Almost there. Come on, we need to dance."

She'd lost me.

She flapped her arms at me. "You must have heard of dancing. You're not that ancient."

"Very funny. Any special requests?"

She rattled off a list of songs I'd never heard about, and some that I had. Dutifully, I created a playlist.

Adriana turned out to be as good as a Ziegfeld girl.

I on the other hand was not. Even with Adriana's best attempts to teach me to "hop down front then doodle back" and dance the Black Bottom, I flailed around like a drunk sailor.

"Not like that." She wagged her finger at me. "Like this. Hands on your hips and do the mess around. Break a leg until you're near the ground."

"I'm sorry." I tried again.

"Yes." She made a small gleeful jump.

"I did it right?"

"Geez, no. But you got it wrong just right. I remember exactly where I saw this Russian dame."

"The Duchess Natalia?"

"Duchess, my foot. Or if she was, she'd come a long way. She was skating around the speakeasies, searching for a sugar daddy."

"Are you sure?"

She rolled her eyes. "She couldn't doodle back if you paid her a million dollars, like you."

"Do you think the groom had any idea?"

"Him? Take a gander at the other pictures. That's one of the show girls they threw in the cooler after the raid where they caught Tommy's old man." The corners of her mouth turned down. Her voice shook. "It was awful. Poor Tommy. I've never seen daddy so livid."

"I thought Tommy was straight as an arrow."

"Sure he was, but his old folks? Would your parents want a crook in the family?"

"Probably not," I admitted. "In-laws who are outlaws are definitely an acquired taste."

I went back to my notes. "This picture is from a few months before the raid. How can you see that's one of the show girls?"

"Her shoes. See the rhinestones on the straps and the heels? The whole troupe had them, especially made." She preened a little. "I make one heck of a gumshoe."

"You do. Shall we tackle the notebooks now?"

I read them out to Adriana. The entries had been handwritten, and they hurt her eyes. Or maybe she only wanted to lounge dramatically, a dainty hand pressed onto her forehead.

I dimly recollected a similar pose in "It Happened One Night". Adriana had a well-developed flair for dramatics, and she deserved to be indulged while we were alone.

Stewart Schuyler had indeed possessed a reputation of being a bit of a man about town, who liked female company of the easy sort. I chuckled at the turn of phrase. His engagement had surprised the town, but delighted his parents who wanted nothing better than an heir and a spare for him to follow in the footsteps of all the Schuyler before them.

He'd met his bride-to-be at the Russian Embassy.

I scratched my head. An aristocrat fleeing from the communists was not very likely to hang around that kind of place, if it existed at all in America in the late 1920s. And if so, wouldn't it have been in Washington? Investigative journalism this was not.

Adriana opened her eyes as I explained my deductions. "The Russian Embassy. I so wanted to go, because it was supposed to be all hotsy-totsy and a bit like a Parisian club but Tommy and my sister said no. She could be such a bluenose."

"The place was too hot to trot?"

She shrugged, still slightly peeved in hindsight. But then these things weren't that long in the past for her, if she'd only come back as a ghost when we met.

Her mood became sunny again. "The Schuylers would have been livid if they had any idea their precious blue-blooded new family member had been whooping it up with wrinkly old marks. They were the most crashing old bores. You should have heard Ma Schuyler when she saw the new hem lines." She tugged on hers which still fell well short of her knees. "The old bat had the nerve to call me shameful. Or did she say shameless? Anyway, good on old Stewart to put a cuckoo in her nest."

"Do you think people knew?"

"Wouldn't that have created a stink! No, I don't think anyone apart from us went to that joint. There were a lot of gin mills much closer to Cobblewood Cove, and cheaper too."

"Did Stewart have any idea you'd rumbled his secret?"

Her jaw dropped. "You think he's the one who bumped me off?"

"He and his new wife had a lot to lose," I said. "As a rich man you can get away with youthful indiscretions, but marrying a woman on the make and passing her off as a true-blue, nobler than thou Duchess? Nobody likes to be played for a fool. Or have to lock up their husband in case their eyes so much as strayed."

"I should have loved to see the wedding."

Except she'd already been dead when the ceremony took place.

I had another question. "Did your sister see the woman?" Because if she had, my theory might have hit a snag.

Adriana leaned closer. "You won't tell?"

I gave her my word.

"Annabelle had to wear specs. Any further away than ten feet, and she couldn't tell your aunt from Adam. Of course she couldn't use them in public."

"And her boyfriend?"

"You could have put Tommy in front of a line of chorus girls without any of them catching his eye. That's how crazy he was about Belle."

Which meant that with Adriana out of the way, Stewart and Natalia's little secret had been safe - until now.

The big question was, had Dahlia and Primrose discovered the stain on their family crest and were keen to wipe it out? They'd been looking at all kinds of documents for their exhibition.

If one of them so much as hinted at the fact that their cherished Duchess should have instead been called "the hostess with the mostest", or that Stewart had engineered Adriana's death, they would be desperate to cover up the trail.

Physically, they were too old and frail to have attacked me and broken into the house, but they had enough money to hire an army of henchmen without having to resort to baked beans to live on.

Was someone already out there, waiting for his opportunity, or had they already found their hidden proof?

My stomach knotted itself up. Maybe the enemy had already wormed his way into my life.

CHAPTER TEN

P rimrose Schuyler opened the door herself. "Oh, it's you." Not the reception I'd imagine.

"I'm so sorry. I should have called."

"Not at all." She snapped her fingers and the manservant materialized so silently it gave me a start. "Huggins, would you please take Ms Darling's box?"

"I wasn't sure if these are the sort of things that would be useful," I said. "But it turns out the burglar took off with all the family letters and photographs up to the 1950s." I let the information sink in.

"How awful. Such a terrible ordeal for you." Her gaze slid towards the entrance as she led me to the yellow drawing room. Inwardly, I patted myself on the back.

Primrose should have pretended harder to be upset on my behalf. She'd also tried to pity the loss of anything of value to local history, even if the stuff consisted of nothing more than wedding pictures or the recipe for my great-great-grandmother's famous chutney, which had been passed down through the generations. Incidentally it had garnered over a hundred likes on my food blog.

Heels clicked on the marble tiles.

"Is he here?" Dahlia burst into the room. Her face fell when she saw me. Somehow I got the impression that my cheerful presence did little to brighten their day.

"What's the matter with them?" Adriana asked.

I shrugged, only to realize how weird that must seem. So, I pretended to have a stiff shoulder and rolled it dramatically.

The sisters sighed in unison. "You must think us very rude, especially after all the trouble you've gone to," Dahlia said. "We were expecting Dr Harper. He should have been here already."

"The doctor? Is anything wrong?"

"Oh, we're fine. A tonic every morning, regular exercise, and a glass of wine with dinner, and you'll live to be a hundred, our mother used to say."

Primrose added, "We're at least trying, aren't we, Dahlia? It's our Petey we're worried about."

"The parrot?"

"He's completely off his food. He won't touch so much as a nibble of pepper, and he's declined his nuts ever since the party."

"He'll be fine." Dahlia patted her sister's hand.

Primrose dabbed at her damp eyes with a lace-edged handkerchief similar to the one Adriana used now.

"You must think we're a couple of silly old women, but we've had Petey since he was hatched, and his mother before him. She was our first real pet, wasn't she, Dahlia?"

Her sister clucked her tongue. "Of course we had horses, and a dog. We don't want Genie to get the wrong impression."

"How old is Petey?" I asked in the same instant that Adriana enquired, "Did he get at the hooch? Our quaker parrot did, and he had the worst hangover." She gave the two women a pat on the arms.

Dahlia shivered. "My blood just ran cold."

"Well, excuse me." Adriana stomped her foot. "I only tried to be nice."

"Did Petey have the chance to try any of the liquor? I've heard of similar cases in which the bird..." I paused.

"Was all hotsy-totsy again," Adriana said.

"The bird fully recovered."

The old ladies exchanged a meaningful look. "The champagne."

The doorbell rang. It had to be feature of this town that it always happened in the wrong moment.

"I should leave you to it," I said, reluctantly. It would be easier to wheedle information out of the sisters while they were distracted, but it also felt callous. I'd be distraught if anything happened to Cleo and she wasn't my cat at all.

"Please stay," Dahlia pleaded. "If you'd be so kind to keep Primrose company until the doctor has finished his examination?"

She bustled off, worry lines etched on her forehead.

Her sister slumped in her chair. "I can't imagine life without Petey. He's bringing so much joy into our lives." Her fingers tore at her handkerchief.

"Tell me about him," I said. "Is he your only family? You don't mind me calling him that, I hope."

She clasped my hand and squeezed it. "That's exactly what he is. He's so clever. Did you know that quaker parrots are the only ones that build their nests out of sticks instead of using a hole in a tree? Petey has done the most wonderful creations in our aviary." Primrose blinked back tears.

"How clever of Petey," I said.

Adriana signaled me to move my purse closer to Primrose. I shook my head imperceptibly. If she literally gave the sisters a chill when she came too close, she might cause Primrose to catch a cold or worse.

While the jury was still out on their involvement with my current predicaments, making them ill was a no-no, guilty or innocent.

"Would you like me to fetch you a drink?" I asked. "Tea maybe, or a medicinal brandy?"

"Thank you, Genie. That's very thoughtful." She rang a bell on a gleaming brass board.

Huggins entered. He must have either hovered nearby, or he held a record for speed-butling.

"Tea," she ordered. "And a few macaroons, I think. Have we offered the doctor a refreshment?"

"We have indeed, madam. Dr Harper is still secluded with Miss Dahlia and the patient."

Quick steps and the sound of a heavy door being opened and closed alerted us.

"Wonderful news," Dahlia exclaimed as she almost ran into Huggins, who was on his way out. "Petey will make a full recovery."

Primrose held her arms out and the sisters hugged. The sight of these two old ladies together made me almost wish for siblings, until

I remembered how viciously my paternal aunts used to fight over everything.

"I'm so glad for you," I said. Adriana nodded her agreement.

"We must thank you." Dahlia turned to me. "Dr Harper confirmed your diagnosis. Someone had indeed let Petey get a beak full of champagne or more. He needs rests, darkness, and the lightest of nibbles, but there should be no ill effects."

The sisters broke into a relieved laugh. "You won't tell anyone, will you, Genie? It'd be mortifying for Petey."

I didn't think the parrot would give a hoot about the neighbors talking behind his back at all, but it meant so much to the Schuyler that I promised on my father's grave. While it was touching to see their affection for their feathered friend, it also proved how much store they set in their reputation.

As if she'd read my mind, Dahlia gave a small titter. "You must find our concern quite foolish. You see, our nephew is prone to making fun of poor Petey, and if he'd hear about it, he might make some cutting jokes."

"Like calling him Pickled Petey?" I bit my tongue. "Sorry, that was rude."

"It's exactly the kind of thing George would say." A faint tinge of peek crept over Primrose's throat and cheeks. "Not that he'd intend to be mean. It's just that he's got such a masculine way to look at affairs, and he's never taken to Petey since the incident."

Dahlia shot her sister a warning glance. "Genie doesn't want to hear our mundane family stories."

"But I do. It makes me feel like I'm part of Cobblewood Cove, and my mother too. She'll want to hear all about it. Does George visit you often?"

"He has an apartment in Manhattan, of course, but most of his weekends are spent here," Primrose said.

"That must be lovely for you, to have his company."

"Naturally, he has his own flight of rooms on the second floor. Men do like their independence, and he's so considerate he never disturbs anyone."

"That's good."

"I'm sorry you missed him," Dahlia said. "He had to leave just before the party."

"He'll be back tonight though," Primrose said. "You must come over for dinner one night soon."

"If you're not too busy with the preparations for the grand exhibition?"

"Good heavens, no. That's all well in hand. And now we should take a peek at your box."

The sisters oohed and aahed over the old dresses. "They're perfect, exactly what we need," Dahlia declared.

"There should be more," I promised. "Are you going to highlight the Jazz age too? I could do with some inspiration for my jewelry design. I thought I'd create a new line and call it Cobblewood Cove Likes It Hot."

The sisters sharply drew in their breath. "You wouldn't make real copies, would you?"

"Not exact ones. It's the basic feel of the period I'm after."

Their behavior still puzzled me as I strolled home. Adriana prattled on about her pets, but I only half-listened. Why had the idea of me copying bracelets and rings upset the sisters? Or did they just say that to hide their dislike of anything to do with the era of Adriana's murder?

Chapter Eleven

Adriana flung herself into a chair. Cleo came out from under the dining table and jumped onto the air of the chair. She rubbed herself against Adriana's shoulder.

"Careful," Adriana warned as she stroked Cleo under the chin. "This shawl came all the way from Paris and I don't want any claw marks on it."

I doubted that would be possible, since it was only the illusion of her garment but thought it prudent to keep that to myself.

Cleo treated her to an innocent stare and a miaow.

"What does she say?" I asked.

"That she wouldn't dream of touching my clothes. Your tatty bathrobe on the other hand . . ." Adriana and Cleo winked at each other.

"I thought it got snatched in the washing machine."

Her face went blank.

"The thing that replaced tubs and washboards."

"That of course is also possible." She picked a whisker off her dress.

I goggled. "Do that again."

"Do what?"

"Or let's try something else."

I put a saucer with milk foam in front of ghost and cat.

Adriana slipped out of one glove and tipped her finger into the foam.

I stopped her before she could lick it. "Show me you finger."

"You're screwy."

"Oh yes?" On her finger glistened a tiny fleck of milk. "Then tell me, what are you calling that?"

She held her hand out to Cleo, and the cat licked Adriana's finger with a happy sigh.

"I'm real again." She jumped up and tried to grab me. For a heartbeat I felt her touch, but that instant didn't last. Her face crumpled. A single tear rolled down her cheek.

"I'm sorry," I said. "You're real to me and to Cleo. And you're getting stronger."

She wrapped herself in her shawl. "I am?"

"If a brick and my company are enough to let you leave the house with me, maybe every little thing connected to you helps a little."

She flitted around the room while I thought about this new revelation. Although this stage of her afterlife was bound to end as soon as we'd solved the crime that had brought her to me, she could have a lot more fun now. Maybe we could even hug for real before I let her go.

"You look sad." She mimed pulling up the corners of my mouth.

"I'm tired, that's all," I lied. I'd grown fond of her, as I'd grown fond of Cleo. I'd miss them both when we all went our separate ways.

"Have some giggle water, that'll get your system going. And open that box," she said and pointed at a wooden box on the mantel.

Inside were hair pins and a velvet ribbon.

She fished out a pin and held it up with a triumphant cry. "See that? It was mine." Her neck muscles strained with effort.

"Put it down," I said. "You need to train."

Her breath came out in small puffs as she lowered the pin.

The last time I'd seen anything remotely as strenuous was at a gym, when I'd tried to press 25 kilo discs, to impress a cute trainer. They came close to killing me. I hadn't attempted anything as foolish again. The trainer hadn't been that cute anyway.

Adriana rubbed her arm. "There must be more of my things in the attic." Her excitement grew. "What are you waiting for?"

The lightbulb crackled. The whole house needed sorting out. Which reminded me that I hadn't checked in with Jolene. After all, it was my fault that she'd been injured. I should at least make sure she was doing okay.

"Hey, Genie," Jolene said as she picked up after the second ring tone. Her voice was strong and clear, a good sign. "I meant to give you a buzz, but you beat me to it."

"You did? How are you?"

"You can see for yourself. Give me ten minutes."

True to her word, she stood on the doorstep without a delay. Her bandaged hand made me wince but she waved it off. "Gives me an excuse to have the old man do a few things for me. And you've met my new assistant."

I had. "Hi, Matt."

Adriana rushed to the mirror and rearranged her shawl as she saw our visitors. She patted her hair into place and signaled me to do the same. I ignored that.

"You look surprised," Jolene said. "I thought you were expecting me? You have shoddy wiring?"

"Right. I had no idea you do that too."

"Honey, we're a one stop shop, and I'm your girl Friday." She gave Matt a gentle nudge with her elbow. "Or rather, we both are."

"I thought you're here for the museum objects." I could sense a light headache coming.

"I am, but--" He and Jolene exchanged a silent communication.

"This one can't say no to a damsel in distress," Jolene said as an explanation. Sadly, enlightenment was not forthcoming, unless this was her cute way of saying that he came to her aid because she and Matt were an item.

He took pity on me. "Jolene's my second cousin, twice removed. She put the Schuylers in touch with my agency."

That explained his concern for Jolene. It also cheered Adriana up who'd finished her grooming and sashayed up to us.

Jolene snapped her fingers. "My toolbox."

"It's still upstairs," I said. "Where do you want to start?"

The fuse box was hidden inside a kitchen cupboard. Jolene pooh-poohed at the location, which was awkward to reach in a black-out. She suggested stick-up lights in a few places. I agreed meekly. If we had another intruder again, the more light, the better.

Jolene ended her inspection in the living room. "There's nothing wrong with your wiring," she said. "You've got more than enough juice, fuses are new, and you won't have to spend a single dime on upgrading anything."

"Oh."

She chuckled. "A customer who's disappointed about saving their cash, that's a new one."

"No, that's awesome news."

"Is it okay to send you the bill tomorrow?" Jolene asked as Matt secured the tools in the box.

"I'll pay it straight away."

Jolene was already out the door, when Matt stopped in the hallway. "I've been meaning to ask you something."

"Fire away?"

"Over dinner?"

Either I'd suddenly become irresistible or there was something in the air, that every eligible man in the area wanted to take me out for a meal. Or did Matt just want to get me out of the house?

Inwardly, I gnashed my teeth.

Adriana fluttered her eyelashes at me.

"How about here," I suggested. "Nine o' clock suit you?"

Jolene called out for him.

"See you later then," he said.

That gave me two hours to throw something in the oven, and to figure out what made the electricity go haywire. Because if the wiring wasn't at fault, something else caused the flickering and crackling. Someone tried to scare me enough to make me leave.

I'd told the sisters the burglar had made off with all the documents the murderer's family could be after, and I intended to feed Fred and Matt the same line. That might throw them off - unless they already

91

knew better. It drove me crazy that I had no clue what form the elusive proof took.

The vegetable lasagna I'd prepared came out of the oven with the cheese golden and the sauce succulent. My nerves vibrated a little as I served it up.

Having a dinner guest who your great-great-aunt was ogling would have been nerve-racking enough. Being in the dark about his possible agenda took the excitement up a few notches. Currently my stress level ranked between upping my deodorant asap and developing an eye twitch.

Matt had brought a bottle of red wine, which made Adriana giddy and added to my tension. On the other hand I could do with a drop, and it might help put Matt at his ease.

He raised his glass in a toast. "Here's to a perfect evening."

We clinked glasses. During the meal - he took a second helping and complimented me! - he admired Cleo who promptly decided to shed on his pants. He laughed it off, a point in his favor.

We retired to the lounge.

I was still on my first glass of wine. This meant I could control my reactions when I saw a gloved hand reach out and fondle Matt's back.

"It is warm here," he said.

Adriana became bolder and squeezed his biceps.

I faked a cough and covered my mouth. She really had a crush on the guy.

"Too hot for you?" I asked, noticing too late the innuendo.

Adriana giggled and wiggled her hips.

"I think I can take it," he said after a moment's hesitation. Either he hadn't taken in my poor choice of words, or he didn't want to flirt with me, or he wanted to spare me embarrassment. Hmm.

I mentally called myself to order. The wine must have gone to my head after all.

"If you're Jolene's cousin, how come you needed her to connect you to Dahlia and Primrose? Or did only Jolene grow up here?" I set a bowl with mixed nuts on the table.

"I'm not sure she counts as local. Her mother married into the hardware store when Jolene was a toddler." He flashed his teeth at me. "But this town suits her. Lots of old houses that cry out for her skills."

"And yours, at least while she's hurt."

"I mostly follow orders. I'd appreciate it if you kept quiet about Jolene and me being related though. Otherwise it can be a bit awkward. Nepotism and all."

"Because you tell people to upgrade security, and they go to her. Gotcha."

Adriana touched his hair. Her giggles grew louder. One more whiff of the wine and she'd enter the hiccup stage.

Matt frowned again. "This house has a peculiar atmosphere."

My eye twitched. "It does? I'll turn down the heating."

"It's not that. It somehow feels welcoming."

Adriana purred with delight. Cleo did the same.

"Maybe it's her." He petted the cat. "That is one special kitty you've got here."

"One of a kind," I agreed.

Cleo put a paw on his hand. He said, "It's almost as if she understands every word."

I changed the subject. "What do you think of Dahlia and Primrose's pet project? It's not as if Cobblewood Cove had a place in the history books. The last exciting thing to happen here must have been when the local courthouse burnt down in the 1900s. Unless you count the infamous speakeasy raid." I helped myself to a glass of water while I watched his reaction. Which didn't come.

"I read about these incidents in the library archive," I said. "It's a pity all our family papers from those eras are gone. I'd promised my mother to keep her informed." A heavy sigh made it clear just how sad the whole affair was.

"I think it's a worthwhile project," he said. "If we don't preserve local history, all we have is the version written by the rich and powerful."

"I never thought of it that way."

"So, maybe a lot of the items wouldn't fetch a dime in an eBay auction, but they're tangible proof of people's lives." He became more animated. "I've discovered a letter from a freed slave to a local woman who helped with the underground railway during the civil war."

"Wow. I can't wait to see that."

"You won't, sadly. Some people are very sensitive to their family's past."

No kidding.

"Ask him if he's got a girlfriend," Adriana hissed in my ear.

I shook my head, no.

Matt gave me a confused look.

I stared back.

"Please," Adriana wheedled.

"I should go," he said. "Thanks for a great dinner."

The lights flickered as Adriana glared at me.

"You're welcome," I said.

"You're a coward." My great-great-aunt stamped her dainty foot on the floor. The lights flickered again.

"Are you mad at me?"

She huffed, and the bulb in the lamp crackled.

I broke into relieved laughter.

"Are you making fun of me?" Her lips wobbled.

"He'll be back. I promise."

"How can you be so sure? He hasn't asked you out again."

I pointed at the floor. There, under the coat rack, lay Matt's monogrammed pen.

She did a quick Charleston step. The light stayed steady.

"You know what's even better?"

Her eyes grew wide. "Is it a secret?"

I inclined my head and lowered my voice to add to the drama. "You can affect electricity."

"I can? That's me?" Her grin came close to splitting her face in half. "I control the power."

"You do. Or you will, with a bit of training." Maybe I should consider myself lucky that Adriana was as sweet-natured as they come. Otherwise I shuddered to think about the havoc she could wreak, the way her powers grew.

95

CHAPTER TWELVE

"Last one up loses." Adriana flitted upstairs while I trudged up behind her. On the upstairs landing, she stopped me from switching on the lights. She pressed her fingertips against her temples.

"What are you doing?"

"Shhh. I need complete silence."

She tilted her face to the sky, or rather the ceiling. "Mmmmhhh."

There should have been thunder rumbling though the air for effect, I thought. I had a ghost, a mystery, and over a century's worth of junk to take care of, so why not crank up the craziness?

Adriana dropped her hands. "It doesn't work. I can't turn on the light."

"Maybe because you're not angry, or excited enough," I said. I regretted my words before I'd even finished the sentence. Too late.

She said, "You've got it, sister. That's how we'll teach me. Bring on the fun."

"Later," I said. "And we should start small. You don't want to be exhausted. It shows in the face."

"I hadn't thought of that. You're a doll."

I wasn't, but if I'd learned one thing about my dear, not quite departed relative, it was that I could count on her vanity. Never mind that I was her only audience. Well, and the cat.

"This is ridiculous," Adriana complained when I'd finished sorting through three trunks of accumulated heirlooms.

All I'd discovered were toiletries and trinkets and clothes that should have been donated while they were of use to anyone. The early Darlings must have been one genome removed from becoming full-blown hoarders.

I pushed the trunks into the remotest corner. The things I'd deemed interesting fit into a carry-on suitcase.

An owl hooted. Twinkling starlight fell in through the skylight. It surrounded Adriana's head with a silvery glow.

"Midnight," she said. "And you'd promised me a fun evening."

I rubbed grime off my hands. "This doesn't count?"

Her shoulders sagged.

"One hour, okay? And then we'll go to bed."

I woke up on the sofa, with a crick in my neck and Adriana standing over me. On the table stood a glass of wine, ready for the two of us to share.

Only now bright sunlight fought its way through gaps in the shutters. I'd slept through the night.

"I thought you'd never wake up," Adriana said.

"I'm sorry." I dragged myself off the sofa, grateful I'd changed into my pajamas for our girls' evening. A liter of coffee and I'd be fully functional. At least I hoped so.

The coffee machine stopped halfway through the brewing process. I hit the button. Nothing. I hit it again.

"Leave it to me." Adriana hummed to herself, a happy little melody that inspired Cleo to fall in with a snuffle. Adriana's natural glow intensified and the coffee machine belched into action.

"Wow."

She gave a modest shrug. "While some of us were snoring their head off, others were busy doing useful stuff."

"I don't snore."

She snorted.

"And I can't help needing sleep. Don't you, I don't know, fade away or whatever at all?"

"No." A tragic lip wobble. "It's awful. I'm all alone, in this big house, listening to you mumble and rustle around. Cleo kept me company for a bit but then she nodded off for ages. So much for cat naps. The best I could do was close my eyes and count sheep. One sheep, two sheep, a million sheep . . . "

"You were bored and lonely."

I added enough milk to my coffee to cool it down enough to take huge gulps. Poor Adriana. The sooner she reached whatever plane it was, the better for her.

"How about we talk now," I suggested. Later, I'd introduce her to a few more movies. They might help keep her entertained during the hours I intended to spend getting enough rest to be more than a zombie. "Tell me about your favorite things."

A dreamy look came in her eyes. "There were so many. Having a new dress, and helping Belle pick out hers. You wouldn't believe how much I had to take care of her clothes. Without me she'd have walked around in jumpers and a skirt all day, and that in the wrong shades." She gave me critical stare, but then I'd never planned for my flannel pajamas to be judged by an early fashionista.

"You should wear peach and gold," she said. "It'll warm up your complexion. You don't want to look like an old spinster, do you?"

Maybe I wouldn't miss her that much after all.

"Although you're naturally pretty," she added. "Like my sister."

Okay, I would miss her.

"You wouldn't believe how beautiful she was on that day." The coffee machine went out. Uh-oh. I needed to steer her away from the subject of this specific date. Reliving her last conscious hours would be enough to stress out anyone, but I wasn't sure how much more anguish my appliances could take.

"What else did you do?"

"The usual. Going to parties and dances. And the pictures. Aren't the theaters the bee's knees?"

"They sure are."

"Of course I was also busy with my typing and stenography classes." My surprise must have shown, because she added in a hurt tone, "That doesn't mean I'm a bluestocking."

"No. I think that's great."

99

"You do? Maybe there's some of my work upstairs. It's a leather-bound diary, with an embossed Primrose."

"I'll search for it later," I promised. "What kind of work is it?"

She twirled. "It's poetry. Like Dorothy Parker? I saw her once, her and her friends, at the Algonquin. She was having a mimosa, and the men would all fall over themselves to get her another drink."

"In public? What about the Prohibition?"

"Silly, they'd call it lemonade or something but I read that she loved her mimosas."

"Three things I shall never attain: Envy, content, and sufficient champagne," I quoted.

Adriana burst into laughter.

"That's one of Dorothy Parker's," I said.

"Don't you just adore her?" She mimed knocking back a drink and slung her shawl around her. "Imagine having all these beaus."

"You surely had a few admirers yourself, you and Belle."

"She never looked at anyone but Tommy, even when she came back from Switzerland. It was love at first sight."

"Did you go to Switzerland too?" A finishing school with the upper class girls from all over the world and typing courses didn't quite add up.

She pushed out her bottom lip. "I would've, except Lucille Ward spoilt it for me when she became a little too keen on one of the lounge lizards in town. She snuck out with him once too often, and she had to pay an urgent visit to an aunt when they came back. A visit that lasted seven months, if you get my meaning. My grandparents thought of finishing schools abroad as dens of iniquities ever since and so, I stayed home."

"Lucille Ward? A relative of the mayor?"

"His niece, and the niece of the Schuylers too. It didn't hurt her too much though, she bagged herself a manufacturer who was lousy with it." She rubbed two fingers together.

"That must have been a scandal."

"If people had gotten wind of it. The only one who was there when Lucille was skating around with her fella, was Belle, and she wouldn't tell anyone. That is, except me and our parents, who decided that I could do without Switzerland."

"That must have been hard for you."

"Well, I didn't exactly break into a song and dance, but like I told Lucille, I wasn't going to hold her taste in men against her."

"You told Lucille that you knew?"

Adriana's mouth set in a grim line. "She shouldn't have said I'd be lucky to find anyone half as good as she, and that Belle's Tommy was a flat tire."

So, the fallen girl had been aware that Adriana posed a threat to her reputation, and possibly her upcoming marriage. Another motive for murder. I itched to find out more about Lucille.

"Would you like to watch another movie while I run a quick errand?" I asked. If I unplugged all other appliances and asked Adriana to resist playing around with the electricity, it should be fine. Having her tag along might have been safer, but she also tended to be a big distraction.

I rummaged around in the DVD collection and we hit upon *Blithe Spirits* by Noel Coward.

"Swell! Daddy took me to see his plays on Broadway," she said. "

"This could be amusing then. I haven't seen it but it's still supposed to be a classic after all these years."

Her voice became small. "Everyone's gone. It's only me left."

"You've got me and Cleo."

I crossed my fingers as I left that the movie would distract her. Exuberance was much better than a blue funk, as understandable as it was.

My phone rang on the way out. Dahlia, with an update on the parrot.

I offered to drop by later with new items and to see the patient. With any luck I'd also see the nephew who was fast becoming my prime suspect.

Chapter Thirteen

B irdsong filled the air and I cheerfully waved left and right to a neighbor mowing his lawn, another pruning his shrubs into a geometrical shape, and a young mother taking her toddler and her pekingese out for a walk.

The little dog yapped at me, and so did a spaniel when I came within 20 yards. Whatever spell Adriana cast over animals clearly hadn't rubbed off on me. On the upside, my shoulder was blissfully pain free. It had its advantages walking around without a cumbersome brick in my purse.

I'd decided against paying the library another visit. If Fred was in cahoots with the villain of the piece or worse, the mastermind behind it all, talking ago him bout an old family scandal or giving away my interest was the last thing I intended.

Instead, I headed towards Gossip central, otherwise known as The Cocoa Cabana. Less than 50 yards away from my destination, a stranger hailed me. "Genie Darling, I presume?"

I confirmed that, yes, that was indeed me. I shook the hand of a woman my own age, with wild hair, snazzy specs in a black and white frame, and a brisk smile.

She also had a name tag clipped to her blouse. It read, Daphne Mills, Head Librarian. "Sorry I missed your visits," she said. "Fred been looking after you okay?" I took to her in an instant, and I hoped she approved of me too.

"Everything's great," I said. "Fred's been wonderful."

"That's good to hear. He spotted you and since I was heading this way, he asked me to give you this."

She handed me another photocopied article and read over my shoulder. "'Love at first sight for beauty queen and her groom'. I'd say his moolah might have helped. Don't you think so?"

"It's possible." For the picture underneath the headline showed a youthful Lucille exchanging a kiss with a balding man old enough to be her father.

Was it coincidence that he should give me this article now? Or had he heard about my trip to the town hall and tried to make it clear that Lucille had been happily wed and there was nothing to see about Lucille's premarital indiscretions?

"You should skip to the bit where one of the bridesmaids elopes with the married ring bearer," Daphne said. "It's an instant classic."

"Did they run off at the wedding?"

"No," she admitted. "But it was close enough to the main event that the connections were clear. The new bride was slightly peeved that somebody stole the attention. But then people could do with a bit of cheering up, everywhere." She grinned at me. "Sorry, I love these little sidebars. They tell you everything you'd want to know about a place."

"Have you any family connections to Cobblewood Cove?" I hoped my question came off as normal curiosity. It would be good to have one possible resource who had no personal interest in covering up anything from the past.

"Does dating and dumping two local guys count? Otherwise, no." She looked around, right at the old ladies with Fred. "Sadly, no. I was so lucky to be offered this position. But I'd better finish my errands and return to my duty."

I entered the Cocoa Cabana, with the intention of striking up a friendly conversation with some of the old ladies who spent half the day upstairs over warm pastries, hot drinks and even hotter gossip.

Alas, it was not to be. I'd barely made it through the door when Jonathan made an appearance. "I thought it was you," he said.

Two old ladies, who were busy handing over their coats to an elderly waitress, gave us an appraising glance. One of them showed a coy smile, while the other one tried to quell her.

I could sense them tick off in their heads a few interesting pieces of information about me.

Age: early 30s, rings on my finger but no wedding band, from one of the better families although raised elsewhere (this should count as a black mark against my name).

I wondered if they hoped I'd make a match with handsome Jonathan, or if they'd already earmarked him for a local woman.

"Mind if I join you?" he asked with just the right amount of good humor and good manners to make the old ladies sidle closer.

"Not at all."

He scanned my reading material. "If you're interested in local folk-lore, I could tell you the really juicy stuff about the Harewoods over a cup of coffee."

I was intrigued.

He winked at me. "Maybe somewhere with a bit more privacy."

The Cocoa Cabana boasted seating in discrete little booths upstairs. This genteel room with its chintz drapes and flowery wallpaper had seen the dissection and demise of more than one reputation.

Aimée had dubbed the process "Death by Devil's Food Cake". That name had stuck in my head, together with the memory of the best pastries and chocolates by a country mile.

At this hour though we decided on coffee and nothing else.

"Spill," I said, after the waitress had put down a silver coffee pot and two cups and was safely out of earshot.

"Are you always this direct?" His eyebrows shot up.

"If I have a lot on my to-do list, yes." I'd promised Adriana a speedy return. By now her movie should be coming close to the final act. "Unless you'd rather not dish the dirt on your family." I fluttered my lashed. "Skeletons in the closet and all that."

"We're not that exciting. Nothing like the Drawing Darling."

"The Dueling Darling, you mean. And it was only one duel, and one Darling." Family lore had it that the first Darling who'd settled in Cobblewood Cove had defended the honor of a beautiful young lady in a match of pistols by dawn against a villainous rake. Both were said to be excellent shots, but justice and my ancestor prevailed.

Thus the Darlings, whose first appearance on this shore had been in the form of a Hessian soldier by the name of Liebling who took to the new country in the twinkle of an eye, had become welcome members of the community and established their standing.

Like most of the newcomers who'd braved the perilous ocean journey, he'd built his house with a sea view from the upper level, yet far enough to feel safe. Only people with a close connection to the sea stayed by the seafront.

"I can't beat that," Jonathan said. "But we Harewoods didn't use to be quite as squeaky clean as we like to pretend. Parts of the family fortune were made by supplying booze during the prohibition."

I oohed in feigned surprise. "Old Harewood was a bootlegger? Moonshine and bathtub gin?"

"Classier than that, if the family stories are to be believed, but close enough. You do know your period terms."

So would anyone who shared the same roof with my great-great-aunt, not that I planned to tell him - or anyone. That way the straitjacket lies. Instead I showed off my jewelry. "It goes with the territory. People who buy my work like to think they're getting a piece of The Great Gatsby with it." I put on a winning smile. "What does classier mean?"

Jonathan's gaze swept around to make sure we really were alone. "Brandy, or rather sacramental wine as it was labelled. Churches and cloisters made a great cover."

"Ingenious," I said. "It would have been impossible to cut off their supply of wine for mass."

"I think so. Of course it's possible the stories have been embellished over the years, like saying he was paid in double eagles as well as plain bank notes, but I for one am a little proud of the old rogue. I hope that doesn't scandalize you. It's not as if he belonged to the mob or murdered anyone."

My laugh came across less convincing than I'd hoped. "At least he's not boring. Does the whole town know?"

"Heavens, no. My grandmother and my mother would have been barred from the Temperance League and the Women's Club, although we were only related to the man through his younger brother. He died during the Great War."

That gave the older generations a motive to keep the booze business as secret, but after a public arrest there wouldn't have been that much reputation to save.

Adriana had confirmed as much. Which reminded me, I had to go. At least I could strike Jonathan off the list, not that he'd ever figured prominently on it. But anyone who tried to cover up a shameful secret would keep his mouth shut instead of telling a stranger.

"You're leaving so soon?" His disappointment flattered me, although he probably only enjoyed having someone to talk to who heard all his stories for the first time.

"You must have things to do yourself," I said.

"Nothing that can't wait."

"Another day? Which reminds me - thanks for sending over that handyman. I would have used his services if I hadn't already arranged something else."

After a moment's pause which lasted just long enough to make me wonder if I'd offended his male pride, he shrugged it off. "I'm only glad your locks are fixed. Jolene's usually in high demand, otherwise I'd have recommended her instead of this man."

"No hard feelings, then?"

"Heavens, no. I barely knew him except that he did a good job for me, on someone's recommendation. George, I think it was."

The waitress bid us a cheerful goodbye. Her glance lingered on Jonathan, understandably. He must be quite the catch in a small town like this - if he was a single as I thought.

He offered to drive me home. For a moment I was tempted. Cars and the clutter inside or lack of clutter tell a lot about people.

Sadly, I'd also feel ridiculous, considering I lived less than a ten minutes' walk away.

Also, one man Adriana had a crush on was enough to deal with. If she decided to upgrade Jonathan from Swell to Sheikh, things might become a little too interesting.

I needn't have worried. Flirtation was the last thing on Adriana's mind. She cowered with Cleo under the sofa throw when I came home. When I saw her face, an inane thought crossed my mind. Now I knew what pale as a ghost meant.

"What's wrong?" I asked. "Did we have another break-in?"

She whimpered. "No. It's worse."

I sank onto the sofa, next to her.

"Tell me."

Her eyes were filled with fear. "They're going to kill me."

CHAPTER FOURTEEN

M y breath caught in my chest so hard it hurt. It would have been more than a little late to fear for Adriana's limbs and life, but she did not deserve to be in a state of panic.

"I'm here now," I said. "You're safe."

"That's what she thought." Tears welled up.

Cleo purred at her.

"What exactly happened?"

She pointed an accusing finger at the DVD sleeve. "That woman came and they had a seance to get rid of the first wife."

"Okay..."

She stared at me as if I'd suddenly grown hooves and reeked of sulphur. "Would you do that to me?"

"What?" Then it dawned on me. "Of course not. It's only a story."

"But what if it's not?" She shook so badly Cleo hit at me. She kept her claws in though.

I got the message. I was not to upset Adriana, or else I was in the cat's dog house.

"It's all made up," I repeated.

"How can you be sure? Maybe Mr Coward had a person who'd passed on, too." She gulped.

I silently cursed myself. I should have been more careful with whatever I exposed her to, especially when it was impossible to prove anything having to do or rather not to do with the realm of spirits.

Up to now I'd been glad Adriana appeared to be the only of her kind hanging around me. Instead I found myself wishing she could receive some guidance and counseling from another ghost. Oh, and me too. A nice, maternal spirit who'd tell us what wonderful things awaited Adriana once she'd fulfilled her purpose.

"I promise you we will keep any medium or other psychic far away from us."

"I need more." She hiccuped. "You would too, if your life was in danger."

"You're right. I'll find out as much as I can."

"You're not leaving me again, are you?"

"Where I'm going, you're going." I held out my hand for a high five which confused her until I explained the concept.

I had the briefest sensation of her touch before her fingers blurred and merged with mine. And, like Matt had said, it felt warm and welcoming.

It took me two trips to the car to load a few pieces of 200 year old furniture into the boot.

The sight of me balancing chamber pots and boot jacks cheered Adriana up. So did the moustache curlers and glove stretchers we'd discovered in a toiletry set.

The not much younger powder puff had been dabbed all over Adriana's face, in a joint effort. She guided my hand and instead of floating around, the tiny grains seemed to settle on her skin.

I gave up figuring out the logic and decided to just go with the flow.

The Schuylers accepted my donations with satisfying gratitude. Dahlia and Primrose sorted through my offerings side by side, dressed like upper class 1950s matrons. "We thought about doing a vintage dress competition," Dahlia told me. "It would be such a shame to keep these pretty clothes in display cases."

"We wouldn't use the fragile items," Primrose hastened to reassure me. "You won't have to worry about your treasures."

"I think it's a great idea," I said in all honesty.

The sisters beamed at me. "Oh, good. We had hoped to convince you to model a dress."

"I could pick something for you," Adriana said. She fluffed her hair in front of the large hall mirror.

"Maybe." One of the rules I'd learnt in dealing with elderly woman was that they had a memory like elephants, and would use every word against you.

A tall man with dark hair shot with silver and a chiseled jaw came bouncing down the stairs. I took him to be in his early fifties, and well-preserved at that.

"You must be the famous Genie." He shook my hand precisely long enough to show his sympathy without being over familiar. His brown eyes showed off his tan, and he wore a tailored jacket to designer jeans.

I could easily envisage him on Wall Street. On Main Street, Cobblewood Cove, he would be the shining example mothers held up to their sons, and the kind of man presented to daughters as a prize. Or maybe that thought flashed through my mind because of Dahlia and Primrose's dresses and their doting glances at him. "George Schuyler, but you will have guessed as much."

"We told George how generous you've been, and how helpful. With the exhibition."

Did I detect a hint of a warning in Primrose's voice? Then I remembered their anxiousness that George would be unaware of the source of Petey's illness.

"You remind me of your mother. How is Amy, pardon, I should have said Aimée? "

"Enjoying her honeymoon."

"Your mother used to babysit George when he was little."

"Not that she was that much older, but George adored her, didn't you?" Primrose chuckled. "I'm sure he had a little crush on her."

A flicker of annoyance flashed up in George's eyes. "I'm sure we'll meet again, Genie. Sorry I can't stay longer."

"You shouldn't have said that," Dahlia admonishes her sister when George had disappeared upstairs. "Gentlemen don't like to be teased."

Primrose's shoulders slumped.

"I'd love to see Petey," I said in an attempt to distract them.

"Of course. This way."

"Finally," Adriana said. "This nephew is a washout. He's old enough to be your granddad."

Petey sat in a large cage that resembled a jungle with golden bars. He perched on a platform next to water and food bowls.

"We try to keep him quiet for a while," Dahlia said. "If we let him out, he won't stop exploring. He's such an adventurer."

Petey lifted his head and said, "Hello."

"He likes you," Dahlia said. "He doesn't easily take to people." She chirped at him.

I could have told her what was going on, but she wouldn't have believed me. It wasn't me Petey had greeted. He'd said hello to Adriana who now stood next to him.

Petey clicked his beak in excitement, while my great-great-aunt held a soft conversation with him. I strained my ears but couldn't make out the words.

"Isn't he a good boy?" His doting owners fondly gazed at him. "Such a good judge of character too. He took a dislike to our new gardener right away, and guess what we found out a little later?" Dahlia asked.

Her sister finished the story. "He stole our plants and sold them to his other customers. Two dozen tea roses and who knows how many geraniums."

"We had to give everyone warning," Dahlia said. "Imagine if we'd have let him into the museum."

"Shocking," I said, and I meant it. Losing your business over a few plants? Hardly the crime of the century, and yet this gardener should have seen what was coming.

Petey shut his eyes, and Adriana returned to my side. I took the chance to excuse myself. I'd come to see the nephew, and I'd done that. He fitted the image I'd had. Outwardly charming, but not to be crossed, or he wouldn't have sent his aunts in a tizzy over a silly comment.

"Would you like me to spill about what Petey told me?" Adriana asked.

"You seemed to get on like a house on fire," I said.

"He's a hoot. He says, the old gals are a soft touch, but George is a tough nut to crack. And he sneaks out through the back door."

"He does?"

"Petey recognizes the steps. The old butler drags his dogs." She caught my confusion. "His feet. The old birds wear heels that click, but George's a flannel foot. Rubber soles on his shoes, says Petey."

"Has he tried them?"

"He's a parrot, they like to nibble."

A lightbulb went off in my head.

"Can you talk to any animal?"

"How am I supposed to know? It's not as if you take me out much."

"I should do that." We stopped outside the garage. "How about we do it now?"

She clutched the purse with the brick. "Are we cracking the case?"

"We're at least trying. There might be a witness we've overlooked."

Her mouth formed an o. "And we'll get him to snitch."

"Not we. You. You're the secret weapon."

CHAPTER FIFTEEN

Wе found the first interviewee in his front yard where he tore the last strips of meat off a bone.

Either Groucho had had enough - the bone didn't seem to be too fresh - or the little dachshund decided that Adriana was much more interesting than a meal he could return to whenever he wanted.

She stroked Groucho's nose and he gave a satisfied little growl. I kept my distance, pretending to admire the display of roses that framed the white gate. Groucho threw himself in front of Adriana's feet, so she could give him belly-rubs.

For a small dog, Groucho had a deep voice. He became so excited that his owner poked her head out the front door to make sure everything was fine.

Adriana giggled, and the dachshund rolled his eyes. She gave me a finger wave to signal she needed a little longer.

I took a step back, and then hurried close to the fence again as Adriana's form became less defined. I needed to figure out how to keep the connection to me and her home stable if I moved.

Maybe the library stocked books on the occult, and maybe some of these books were right on the money when it came to the treatment of ghosts.

Groucho at least knew exactly what to do with specters, or at least with this one. He tried to lick her hand.

Adriana petted him again and dragged herself away from him, with so many sorrowful looks that I hoped Cleo would never find out about her canine competition.

"What did he say? Did he see anything?"

She tapped her nose. "He gave me a name."

I punched the air. "Yes."

A woman cycled past. Or rather, she'd planned to, but my exclamation made her stop. "Excuse me? Were you calling me?"

"Sorry," I said. "I'm rehearsing. Amateur theatre, and I got carried away."

"I didn't know there's a new production." She moved closer and lowered her voice. "Are the auditions still on?"

"It's not a local group," I hastened to say.

She lightened up and cycled away.

"Can we scoot now?" Adriana asked.

I followed her meekly, until we reached the alley leading to our own back yard. Although it wasn't directly overlooked, one mansion sat at a strategically placed corner, and in the yard a boxer rested outside a dog house.

"This is Fifi," Adriana whispered. "She's supposed to have the best nose and the best memory in town."

Which also meant that Fifi sniffed me out in a New York second and barked. I couldn't slink off and leave Adriana, for obvious reasons, but it took me a lot of willpower.

"Shush," Adriana said.

"I didn't say a thing."

"Not you." She hummed at Fifi, and before I could so much as catch my nerve, the fearsome guard dog had turned into a softie.

"You stay right behind me," she said to me. We moved close enough that Adriana stood inside the yard and I kept on the safe side of the stone wall.

The interview took longer than with Groucho.

I resigned myself to scroll through my emails when Adriana tore herself away from her new friend.

She fizzed with excitement, and the street light that had just come on, blew its bulb.

I really needed to find a way to prevent that before she plunged the town into a blackout.

For once Adriana kept quiet until we were safely home. She didn't have to say anything anyway. Her self-satisfied smirk gave her away. And the fact that she floated a few inches above the ground, making her taller than me.

"I need something to wet my whistle," she announced as she dramatically draped herself over the sofa.

"This isn't a bar, and I'm not a bartender." I congratulated myself on my firm stance. If I didn't set boundaries, she'd soon walk all over me. It was bad enough that Cleo considered me to be a push-over (confirmed by the feline lady herself, I'd been told). The last thing I needed was another relationship of that sort.

Adriana pouted.

"You can have a cappuccino," I said.

"With sprinkles?"

She could take in about one drop of coffee-infused milk and a single grain of chocolate powder but she loved it, with a capital l. Her words.

I agreed. "You can tell me while I make the drink."

"Fifi says she saw a man skulking around the back yards on the fateful night. A brute of a man, with a sinister look on his face who had no business being where he was, or she would have recognized his smell." she said. "He reeked of wrong-doing."

I mentally erased the overly dramatic statements. "Did she say anything else? Could she describe him, or give us anything to work with?"

"Only that she saw him again. And smelled him." She wrinkled her nose. "She said he was dressed in an almost fur, that whiffed of gas."

That didn't tell me anything.

She gave me a pitying look which I declined to react to in any way.

"The kind of funny thing the chauffeurs wear when they tinker with an automobile," she said.

"A coverall? When did she see him?"

"A couple of runs around the tree before the red-haired woman who's always good for a biscuit or two pulled up. I think she meant Jolene."

I'd gathered as much. Which made the man in the coveralls our burglar suspect, and I had a name for him. When he called to fix the locks he'd picked himself in the first place, the name had been Bert.

The plot thickened.

CHAPTER SIXTEEN

"How are we going to make the louse sing like a canary?" Adriana asked. "Do you have a bean shooter? Then you could tell him either he opens his big fat flab or you'll clip him."

I opened one eye.

My great-great aunt's eager face hovered a few inches above mine.

"Go away and let me sleep," I groaned. I'd only just closed my eyes, or so it felt after half a dozen interruptions by Adriana.

"You said that already and I did leave you alone."

"For about two hours."

"Cleo's hungry. You can't let her starve."

She made way for me to swing my legs out of bed. The cat rubbed herself against me, in anticipation of breakfast.

Adriana prattled on. "Do you think you should call those two police officers in on the case? Or can we nab him on our own?"

"What are we going to say? A trusted source told us who might be the man who broke into our house, you know, the case you didn't even believe existed?"

She gasped. "He must have been the one who attacked you too. Geez."

"It's likely," I admitted.

"So, what's our plan?"

"Have breakfast and pay a visit." I left it at that. If she'd asked me for details, Adriana's belief in our sleuthing skills would suffer a serious blow. I had no idea what I would do.

She whizzed around like a child on a sugar rush as we stepped out onto the mean streets of Cobblewood Cove, this recent hotbed of crime.

"Slow down," I said after I'd hit myself with my purse hard enough to expect a fist-sized bruise or worse.

"You're a drag," she complained.

"Would you rather stay home?"

She changed to a snail-like pace. "I'm fine. I need to say hello to my friends anyway."

With the dogs greeted in an effusive manner, we made our way towards the Harewood residence. If my visiting the town's most eligible bachelor sent tongues wagging, so be it.

I needn't have worried.

Jonathan stood outside the local bookstore as Adriana and I turned onto Main Street. Unruffled and handsome enough to draw a whistle from Adriana, he was browsing the same collection of newspapers I'd started with.

He waved at me as Adriana ogled him with every sign of approval. "You've inspired me to find out more about my ancestors," he said.

"And what did you discover?"

He grimaced. "Next to nothing, apart from the infamous raid. It's like he led a charmed life. Or the editor had an idea the old man's days were numbered and didn't want to mire the family in scandal just then." He motioned towards the bookseller inside. "I've ordered a couple of books on local history. Maybe they'll have more."

"Did you ask the librarian?"

"I prefer to buy books. Keep the local economy going."

"I agree."

"Do you want to continue your research?"

"Actually, I came to find you." I treated him to a lighthearted smile. "Do you have an address for the handyman you sent me after all?"

He took a step back. "Is anything wrong? I've heard that Jolene had an accident."

"She's okay," I said.

"I'm glad to hear that. But why do you want to hire someone else?"

I debated with myself. "I think he was the one who broke into my place," I said. "I found a cigarette paper in the hallway. At first I didn't think anything about it, but somehow my gut tells me it could be a clue. Because, honestly, how many people still smoke?"

"I'm impressed," he said.

So was I, because I'd made things up. There was no cigarette paper, but given the nicotine stains it sounded plausible enough to me. Adriana winked at me.

Jonathan produced a small case that held dozens of business cards. He flipped through them. "I thought I put his card here. Sorry, I'll have to search at home. And check my locks too, if he really is a criminal."

"I'd appreciate that."

"Criminal?" Dahlia Schuyler's brows puckered as she stepped out from the bookstore. She had Matt in tow. He cradled a stack of books.

"I asked Jonathan if he'd read about this one case in the news," I improvised while I beseech him silently.

Jonathan confirmed my words.

"He likes you," Adriana said while she scrutinized both him and Matt in turn. I needed to find her a better outlet for her emotions. I'm sure she came close to committing harassment.

"I'd better run," I said. "I'll see you all soon."

Jonathan winked at me and mimed phoning me. I had an ally.

"And now?" Adriana asked.

"Now we'll do what we should have done already. We'll search the house for anything remotely connected to you."

She made a windmill with her arms. "Oh, goody. I'm sure there must be heaps."

While I waited to hear from Jonathan, we did a sweep of the complete attic. In Adriana's days, it had housed two maids and the cook. A later Darling had taken out the partition between two of the rooms and tuned it into a playroom for the nursery before it became storage.

The late Lottie had used only half the rooms on the two family floors which meant more for us to search. Adriana insisted on directing me. After all, she'd spent all her life in the house, and she swore she remembered every inch of it.

Secretly, I considered that a gross exaggeration. If she'd ever set foot in the kitchen, it had been to ask cook for something.

At least she took her changed surroundings in her stride. The only thing that fazed her was the microwave, after she'd caused a bowl of soup to erupt with her wave interference trick.

The attic had yielded a tennis dress, a blouse, and a cigarette holder Adriana had used as a prop for a costume ball. "There must be more," she said. "Where's all my good clothes? And my choker? I always wear it with this dress."

"We did find the dress and the shawl. Maybe your parents donated the rest," I suggested. "Many people do if someone dear to them passes away."

She glared at me. "Stop talking as if I'm dead." I shut up.

We continued in a subdued mood through the room where quilts and tapestries had taken over any visible surface.

Cleo had done a thorough search first, in the hope of finding and besting a mouse. Considering that her experience as a hunter came down to chasing a few leaves on a covered patio, we were all secretly relieved when she grudgingly gave the room the all clear.

Adriana's mood soured even further when I'd piled up the quilts outside the door and she faced a threadbare rug in pink and purple on the wooden floor. She huffed about the wallpaper as well, which had been updated in the 1970s.

I had to admit it hurt my eyeballs too. Neon-colored swirls appeared to have been free painted onto the striped paper. Great-aunt Lottie in her experimental period had struck.

"That woman better not cross my path," Adriana muttered. "Belle would have hated it. She used to have the sweetest chairs and dresser here, and a four poster bed." We both stared at the divan I'd uncovered. The best thing it had going for it was that it could be thrown out of the window.

"We should look in your room," I said, in the hope to distract her. I expected her to sashay to the airy bedroom where I'd carried all her belongings. It seemed perfect for her, with all the charm of the 1920s, and untouched by Lottie or anyone else.

Instead, she took me to my own bedroom and kneeled on the floor. I squatted next to her as she tried to pry loose a floorboard.

"This was your room?" A sick sensation crept up in my throat. Adriana had died in her own bed. Which might be the one I slept in, the one she hovered over every morning. I had to change rooms. And furniture.

"No, of course not. This was our nursery." She tapped on the floor. "Take it up."

I knocked on the parquet. "It does sound hollow here. Wait."

A paring knife worked wonders as a lever. Hidden underneath the bed, I uncovered a large box inlaid with mother-of-pearl, that fit snugly between concrete and flooring. It must have been built on purpose. At least I did not see two small girls digging a hole in the foundation and covering it up expertly.

"Open it," Adriana ordered.

Inside, under a layer of tissue paper, lay a dozen magazines with covers straight out of a film noir. "The *Black Mask* was my favorite." Adriana's eyes sparkled. "Or maybe *The Detective*. They're both top-notch yarns."

126

That explained her slang expressions which sometimes reminded me more of gangster movies than of a young woman who'd been brought up quite sheltered, as modern for her era as she was. She picked up the uppermost copy.

I stared, open-mouthed. She seemed perfectly unaware of what just happened.

"Do I have a smudge somewhere?" She dropped *The Detective* and ran a finger over her nose and cheeks. Then her jaw dropped too. "Geez Louise."

"Maybe a couple of these things are enough to stabilize you outside the house." I would have done anything to stop carrying that brick around. It made my shoulder and neck hurt.

"Let me look at them."

Obediently, I fanned them out.

"These two are the best. I swear you won't catch a wink until you've finished reading them." She fluttered her long lashes at me. "You could read them to me."

I gave her a non-committal smile and picked up the two magazines.

"Don't," she said in an exasperated tone.

"But I thought--"

"I've seen inside your purse. Breath mints and lipstick! You can take my least favorite copies and stuff them inside. Although they're all super."

My phone rang while Adriana still made her selection. It had to be Jonathan with news. I caught my breath as I answered. "Hello?"

"Genie, sweetheart." Definitely not Jonathan.

"Hi, Aimée," I said, dubiously. "Is anything up?"

Silvery laughter not unlike Adriana's peeled through the receiver thingy. "Everything's marvelous. We've seen dolphins and seals and turtles, and the sunsets are the most beautiful pink and oranges."

"Sounds wonderful," I agreed. "And you're taking time off on your honeymoon to call me because?"

"Tony had the most delightful idea when we had our aperitif." Again, her silvery laughter rang out.

I braced myself.

Tony Novak had many good points, and he made a good match for my quicksilver mother. But somehow I doubted that any plan concocted over what I assumed to be more like a bottle of Dom Perignon than a small glass of sherry would knock me off my feet.

"He thought we could come live in Cobblewood Cove when we're not traveling and make it a happy home again, after all that tragedy."

My mouth fell open. Cobblewood Cove was the kind of place that's perfect for a happy childhood, becomes the place you can't wait to escape when you grow up, and now Aimée had reached the stage where she appreciated its coziness again.

Heck, even I felt the allure.

Some towns are gorgeous on the outside and hollow on the inside. Cobblewood Cove instead was the brick, mortar, and clapboard equivalent of a bubble bath, soothing, and relaxing, and something to long for on stressful days.

I stopped myself before I signed on the dotted line of my imagination and promised to never budge again.

What was going on? I was Genie Darling Hepner, only offspring of two adventurous people.

I'd moved countries more often than I had fingers on one hand. Aimée and me didn't settle per se, we had delightful interludes.

She interrupted my thoughts. "You could have your own apartment in the villa and a studio in the garage. We'll drop by as soon as we're back from our honeymoon, and then we can talk it over. But what do you think?"

I thought that I had been wrong.

Tony's idea was enough to make me break out into sweat. Their honeymoon lasted five more days. I had to make sure that everything was safe for Aimée.

No way was I willing to risk an attack on her.

"I understand that's a lot to take in," she said. "But to also means I'll be in town for the grand evening at the museum. So, if I'm needed in any capacity, like cutting a rope . . ." Her sentence trailed off.

"I'll tell Dahlia and Primrose," I promised. "By the way, do you remember their nephew? You were supposed to have been his babysitter."

She squealed with delight. "As if I'd forget George. Such a sweet boy. He used to give me roses which he stole from the Ward's garden."

That corroborated his aunt's idea that he'd had a crush on Aimée. Somehow I doubted that that old flame burnt strong enough to prevent him from arranging a nasty surprise for her, if she stood in his way.

George Schuyler had come a long way from helping himself to someone's roses to impress a girl.

She made kissing noises to say goodbye although those might as well have been directed at Tony who'd just called her name in the background.

"More family," Adriana said with a critical undertone. "It might get a little cramped in here."

"With six bedrooms?"

Adriana thought again. "Maybe not. But you'll tell her to keep out of my room."

"Tell her yourself. If I can see you, odds are, she can too. She's closer related to you than I am."

My great-great-aunt broke into a face-splitting grin. "And you swear she ain't a drip?"

I quelled her with a haughty stare.

"Sorry," she mumbled. "She's your mom so I guess she's okay."

"Thank you."

She flipped over a page in *The Detective*. She groaned with the effort but after an agonizing ten seconds she managed. "Will you look at that," she exclaimed, glowing with satisfaction.

I gave her a round of applause. "Now you can read for yourself."

"Not so fast. This is heavy work." Hard breathing underlined her words.

"Practice makes perfect."

"You're mean."

I was. But it had been Aimée and me for so long that the only one allowed to make fun of my mother was me, and I intended to keep it that way. Although odds were, she and Adriana would never meet and Aimée would be safe from harm.

I softened. "One short story, at bedtime, if you stay out of my bedroom in the mornings."

"And another talkie. A funny one."

"Deal."

130

I slipped the two magazines she'd chosen into my purse and set the brick on the hallway table before I opened the door. She kept effortlessly by my side as I stepped out. Bingo.

A cluster of neighbors chatted away among themselves on the other side of the street. I gave them a cheerful wave, until I saw their worried expressions.

Something was definitely wrong in Cobblewood Cove.

I moved closer, only to back away as I caught a sentence.

"The police say it was an accident," an elderly lady said.

Her friend blew out her breath. "Too lazy to open an investigation, I bet. I heard he had his neck broken."

"It could have happened when he ran his car into the ditch," a man chimed in. "You watch too many crime shows."

The first woman gave him a pitying look. "Since when did anyone have more than a fender-bender on that back road? My two year old grandson could climb out of the ditch. If you ask me, we're looking at foul play." She tapped her walking stick in a meaningful way.

I pricked my ears. Foul play? But who had died?

CHAPTER SEVENTEEN

W e hot-footed it to the fountain at the square. The Cocoa Cabana and the other café in town were excellent sources of information if I had hours to spare. Today I needed information fast, and the benches around the fountain should be filled with residents only too happy to share whatever knowledge they had.

My calculations were correct. The only thing I'd forgotten were angry clouds darkening the sky and chasing my sources away. I'd have to make do with the library, again.

Then again, any news made its way there, and possibly it would have already been stripped of half the embellishments. Librarians have an inbuilt radar for that.

Fred listened to yet another young mother as he put away children's books. He'd barely made a dent in the stack on the roll cart, so he'd be busy for a little longer.

Adriana waved her hands at the woman. "Shoo."

The woman pulled up her shoulders. "How do you stand the draft?" She took her toddler's hand. "I don't want us to catch cold. Kindergarten sends them home if they're too sniffly."

"I'll have your books stamped in a jiffy, and we have the heating on in the kiddie corner," Fred said and ushered them to his desk. He pressed a button.

Daphne popped her head out of her office and spotted me. "Hey, Genie. You ready to move in here?"

"It does feel like it," I said. "Actually, I'm here to escape the weather." In an aside, I added, "There was talk about a bad accident. I hope nobody got hurt?"

"A man. First fatal accident in a couple of years. It only goes to show how lucky we've been."

"Anyone I know? I don't mean to pry, but somehow..."

"Yeah, I'm the same. From what I've heard, it must have been a stranger, because nobody knew the truck. All I've heard is that he had his work gear in the back, and the police got his first name from that. It's a start."

My stomach lurched.

"First name?"

"A guy called Bert, apparently. But I mustn't stand here, yakking away." She eyeballed me. "You're as white as a sheet. You need to sit down."

Meekly, I sank onto the padded chair in the reading nook and took a couple of deep breath.

If Bert was dead, I had sent the killer on his trail. Both Dahlia and Matt had overheard me asking Jonathan about the man he'd sent. The

133

old lady only needed to mention it to her sister and George would get wind of it. Bert's death was my fault and mine alone.

I bit my knuckles.

Adriana sat beside me and held my hand. "Maybe he was behind the eight ball and he got blotto. Or his automobile blew something. It happens a lot." She clapped a hand in front of her mouth. "They did away with him the way they bumped me off?"

"It could be a coincidence," I said as quietly as I could.

Deep down I doubted that. More likely, our villain had taken a leaf out of a well-used playbook. Maybe they handed these tricks downs the generations, like family recipes for tried and true demise.

I had another thought. If Adriana had come back for us to solve her own case, maybe Bert would return as a ghost too, if the police let the culprit get away.

The question was, how long would that take, and would Adriana be able to talk to him? Would I even want that?

Daphne brought me a glass of cold water and the folio.

I took a deep swig. "It's a long shot, but do you have any non-fiction books on the occult? Ghosts and hauntings and such?"

"Why, is there a specter going around in your attic?" Her question gave me a start. Why was she asking that?

"I can search through our catalog," she offered. "I hadn't taken you for a paranormal hunter."

Until a few days ago, I wouldn't have thought so either. I managed a wan smile. "It's something my mother asked about. Not that she believes in the occult, but there are these old gals in the hotel she's staying at..."

"I know the type. Leave it with me."

As she bustled away, I drew a deep breath.

Who'd have thought that Daphne would be willing to accept a lame reason like this? Luckily, Aimée tended to remember only the important things, and overhear everything not on her radar.

I seemed to have inherited that trait, because it took me by surprise when Adriana broke out into a piercing wail.

My heart sank as she sobbed, "You do want to get rid of me."

"Never," I feverishly wrote in a piece of paper and showed her. "But maybe there's a way to communicate with B."

Adriana calmed down and I crumpled the note and stuffed it into my purse, out of prying eyes. Eccentric behavior tended to be a hot topic and I'd rather not become labelled as the dotty Darling, who wrote herself notes and muttered to herself.

The dark clouds disappeared with the same speed they'd arrived. I left the library with a book about haunted houses and a scientific tome about the afterlife.

Adriana dragged herself alongside. Despite her brave show she obviously still feared that something bad awaited her. The thing was, maybe it did. What if helping her pass on sent her to a fate worse than death? It's not as if could read yelp reviews and make an informed decision.

There had to be a way to bring love, light, and levity into our day. All I could think of was showing Adriana that being a happy, fulfilled ghost had its own rewards, and that in a way she'd believe.

I searched through Lottie's film collection again, until I hit the jackpot. If *Topper* didn't serve as the perfect antidote to gloomy ghost syndrome, nothing would.

Meanwhile, I skimmed through the books.

135

"Will you look at him." Adriana ogled the dashing Cary Grant with all the signs of being smitten.

I had to agree with her. His rakish charm got me too.

There was a sticky moment, when the car Cary and his wife were in crashed, and they both ended up as ghosts, but Adriana barely blinked. Instead, she focused on Constance Bennett, who played the wife. She did bear a striking resemblance to my great-great-aunt, who obviously already saw herself in the role of Mrs Cary Grant.

"He is the absolute cat's meow," she marveled. "Now him I wouldn't mind having around."

This did not bode well for Matt, but if he had any idea about her rapidly dwindling crush on him, he probably would survive the disappointment.

Adriana eyed the finest evening wear made in Hollywood with keen appreciation. "Do you think a long frock would suit me?" Then she cast a not quite as keen glance over my jeans and shirt and shook her head in a resigned manner.

My personal fashion sense had yet to win her over.

A witty line from Cary Grant distracted her. She giggled. Cleo jumped up onto the sofa and squeezed herself in right between us. She too watched the debonair actor with the air of a connoisseur.

When the movie ended, Adriana wafted around, dancing a foxtrot with an imaginary partner. She practically purred with delight.

A crazy thought shot through my head. What if we gave up our investigation? Being back on earth meant a lot to Adriana, and it certainly didn't entail any hardship on her part. I'd be fine with her sticking around too, if she learned to respect my beauty sleep and my privacy.

Then I remembered the dead Bert, and the maybe not so harmless attack on me.

This wasn't a game. I'd simply have to believe that the next step in the afterlife would be heaven, literally.

Cleo left the sofa and curled up on a stool underneath the family tree picture. I'd put it there to see if I could clean it a little and maybe offer to the Schuylers. It should be a great addition to their exhibit.

Armed with a soft cloth and q-tips, I set to work, only to stop dumbstruck when I'd removed soot from Adriana's name and the one next to her.

My mother's words came back to echo in my ears. She mentioned a tragedy. I'd assumed she'd alluded to Adriana's sad story, but there was more.

Belle Darling had died the same month, only a few days after her sister.

CHAPTER EIGHTEEN

I stifled a gasp. No wonder Aimée had mentioned the word tragedy. Two sisters, both dead before they reached the age of twenty-three. I glanced at Adriana who whooped with laughter at Cary Grant's antics.

I decided to keep Belle's death a secret. If she'd been bumped off as well, Adriana would have known. They had been too close in life for anything else, plus I'd have to deal with two specters instead of one.

Nevertheless, I needed to discover more about Belle's story. For that, I had to keep Adriana out of the way. The tricky part was how to manage that without hurting her feelings.

The answer came to me in a rare flash of brilliance. All I had to do was make her decide to send me on an unloved errand. If the Darling sisters had been contemporaries, I could have browsed the internet and found out more about them than anyone should ever be allowed to see (or read), but alas, they'd lived during the long gone glory days of privacy.

"We're out of cat litter," I declared as the final credits rolled. "And of chicken liver for Cleo."

She wrinkled her nose in disgust. "That's so smelly. You can't give her that."

"Instructions from my mother. Liver once a week, beef or chicken every second day, alternating with fish."

She whispered into Cleo's ear. The cat gave her a resigned miaow.

"Be quick, then," Adriana said. "Cleo says she wants it over with."

I grabbed my car keys on the way out. I had no idea if Adriana's senses had been as keen when she was alive, but these days she could have moonlighted as a perfumer's nose.

The sisters lay side by side on Cobblewood Cove's old cemetery.

It broke my heart to think about the poor parents, burying one daughter, only have to say goodbye to their remaining child before the month was out.

I wondered why I'd never heard of that story. Maybe it was too bleak to talk about.

I'd decided to give the library a miss. I couldn't pop in and out, focusing on the same things, without raising suspicion.

On the other hand, if I cast my net too wide I'd be stuck with my nose in the old newspapers until forever. The Cocoa Cabana was out, too. Its customers would be too distracted by Bert's death to be bothered about anything that happened a couple of generations back.

I counted my lucky stars that there was another place where I could tap into the local history. So far I'd ignored the hairdresser's, because the owner's purplish beehive had scared me even as a child. Over the years I'd seen Miss Lola's fascinated stare when she spotted my

139

untamed mane too often to enter her threshold without my blood running cold.

It still had that effect on me.

Miss Lola beamed at me with the enthusiasm of the true, dyed in the wool beauty lover, even if her taste got stuck in her long ago youth.

"I'm sure glad to see you, sweetie." Her eyes behind the thick-rimmed glasses sized me up as she put the finishing touches on one client. She teased another strand high enough to add five inches to the shrunken body of one of Cobblewood Cove's oldest residents, who must have been well over 80 years.

Miss Lola herself was no spring chicken, and she catered almost exclusively to the older generations at *Goldilocks*. One of them sat with her hair in tin foil under the dryer.

Miss Lola nodded to a chair. "If you can wait a little, I should be able to squeeze you in. How about some nice color and a bit of volume at the top?"

I backed away. "Sorry, I've already got my appointment booked back home. It would feel so disloyal if I let her down." A simper accompanied my little white lie.

"That is sweet of you," she said, after she'd digested the disappointment. "You wouldn't believe some of the styles I've seen people come back with after a vacation. I always say, if you've got your hairdresser and your dentist sorted, you're set for life."

"So true," I agreed. "Actually, I was hoping you could help me with something. You know everything there is to know about this town, my mother says."

"Dear Amy. How is she? Married a typhoon, I've heard."

140

I didn't bother to mention the new spelling of my mother's name. Or to correct Miss Lola at all. Typhoon wasn't such a bad description of my stepfather. Kind as Tony was, he created a whirl wherever he went.

"She's fine," I said. "It probably sounds silly, but I'm trying to figure out what I should donate for the exhibition and what I should keep."

"Isn't it exciting?" Miss Lola giggled. "I've heard all kinds of people from all over the state are coming to the opening."

"About time too we get some recognition," the old customer said. "We've had some pretty darn interesting things happening." She lowered her voice. "My gramps swore there's gold hidden on the grounds of the old speakeasy."

Something stirred in my memory. I shoved it aside for now.

"The town history really is fascinating," I enthused. "I've discovered so many things I'd never heard of before." My shoulders slumped in preparation for my next works. "So sad too. Take my own family tree. Two young sisters, and both passed away in the same month, back in 1929."

"A tragedy, that's what it was, Adriana and Annabelle being taken so soon," the old lady said. She touched her hair with a heavily veined hand. "You missed a spot there, Lola."

"I was going to get to it," Miss Lola said and returned to the teasing.

"Can you tell me anything about the sisters?" I asked eagerly.

"You've come to the right person. My mother-in-law's mother was in service with the Darlings." The customer checked her hairdo again. "You couldn't ever get the old lady to set foot in a car, after that."

"Why was that?" Miss Lola asked, saving me the trouble.

"Because that's how they all went. First the youngest, and then, when the sister and her boyfriend drove home from the funeral, his car crashed into a tree. He died at the scene. The girl held on for a little longer, but the doctors couldn't do anything to save her, my mother-in-law said."

My head spun. Another fatal car accident. Maybe I should steer clear of my vehicle.

"You give my love to Amy," Miss Lola said. "And if you ever feel like having a light trim before the big event..."

It took me a couple of instants to realize she meant the exhibition. "I'll keep it in mind," I promised as I headed for the door.

Adriana waited with the air of a martyr when I returned. "That took you forever."

I lifted the shopping bag with my alibi. "I had to hit three shops to find some fresh chicken liver."

"You really should have a maid to do that kind of thing. Or have them send the errand boy."

"We don't want any strangers, remember?" I cut the liver into scraps and put them in a fresh food bowl. Cleo's resistance lasted all of then seconds before she tucked in. "I wasn't gone that long."

There was a gilded wall clock, but that had stopped working in my childhood. I could offer that to the Schuylers, if the need for another visit arose. Anyway, actual time should be immaterial to someone in Adriana's condition. If an hour or two bothered her, how would she deal with eternity?

"Long enough to miss my best trick yet." She allowed herself a hefty dose of smugness. "I've switched on the lights."

I whirled around. Apart from daylight, I couldn't see a single blazing bulb. Or one that had died.

"Upstairs," she said. "Cleo and I have been sleuthing around."

True enough, every single light on the second floor burned.

Adriana collapsed onto a chair after she'd shown me.

"Can you switch them off?"

She shrugged. "Once I've recovered a little, maybe. It's not as if I only need to do this." She snapped her fingers and the lights went out. We stared at each other in awe.

"I'm golden." She snapped her fingers again, and again. It worked like magic. Just like her words.

Jonathan had mentioned double eagles.

The old lady had spoken of buried treasure.

What if they both were right, and Tommy's dad had been paid in gold coins for his illegal services? If Tommy had found out and written a note to Belle, or better still, left a coin with her, that would explain what Bert had been searching for. Back in 1929, a double eagle would have been worth 20 dollars.

Today, they could fetch hundreds of thousands, and the rarest of them went under the hammer for a few cool millions.

To some people they were worth killing for.

CHAPTER NINETEEN

Adriana promised to keep her excitement in check as we drove to the site of the old speakeasy. She'd prepared carefully, because the more of her old belongings Adriana put on, the more power she had. It made sense that she could draw strength from things connected to her original timeline, I decided, as odd as it looked to see her swathed in a shawl on top off an evening frock, with opera gloves, cigarette holder, a bangle in form of a snake and a headband straight out of the Great Gatsby.

I'd expected the joint to be located in one of the less affluent areas of town, close to the water, considering the puritan mindset of that era. Instead, we found our destination on Jefferson Avenue.

The upper part of the mansion had been converted into offices. The basement and first floor still housed a bar.

"What are you waiting for, a written invitation?" Adriana asked.

I tore myself away from the door bells, and the name of the occupants. Among them was Schuyler Holdings.

Adriana circled the downstairs area.

For once, I followed her. It made her exploration easier, and with a Virgin Margarita in my hand, I could easily just be satisfying my curiosity.

The decor had been updated, but not so much that the old character had been lost. Red plush, oak wood and foxed mirrors held a prohibition era vibe, although the cluster of bullet holes behind the tiny stage didn't convince me.

If someone had sprayed the wood paneling in a repeat of the Valentine's Day Massacre, people would still be talking about it.

I took it that one of the subsequent landlords had taken the liberty to embellish the bar's bona fide as a place of infamy and excitement.

Somewhere in the last decades that message must have gotten lost. Three customers in cheap business suits and a bartender who wouldn't see fifty again did not make for lively company, although one of the men did try to hit on me with all the grace of a caveman, until his companions told him to give up and have another beer.

Of course I could also be a little premature in my judgement. Maybe the place was hopping when happy hour came around on Mondays, Wednesdays, and Fridays, but somehow I doubted it.

"What a dump," Adriana said. "Let's go home."

I agreed. Being alone with her and Cleo was a lot more fun.

Adriana, with Cleo in tow, decided to test her new powers over the power in every single room. She whooped with delight as the lights went on and off without fail.

I trailed after the giddy duo, trying to figure out my next steps.

If only I could be sure if all this was about destroying evidence of a killer in the family, no matter if said person had long since left the land of the living, or about money?

Had it been necessary to silence Bert, because I'd fingered him for the break-in or because he had discovered the key to a fortune?

The idea that his death had been simply an unfortunate accident convinced me even less than it had convinced the woman who originally floated the idea of foul play. If only I had a way to get access to the police file.

The two officers who'd answered my call about the burglary had been anything but impressed by my story, and my person. They'd laugh me out of the building if I went there.

I face-palmed, to Adriana's astonishment who instantly tried out this novel (to her) reaction and enjoyed it no end. I knew exactly who I could talk to.

Jolene's hand was still bandaged as she came to pick up her check. She waved off my concern. "As long as there are no other nasty surprises waiting. You wouldn't believe half the stuff I've been seen in houses."

"There's a lot of accidents lately in town," I said in an oh so artless aside. "That man who died in the ditch, for example."

She gave me a shrewd glance.

I decided to come clean, not only because she inspired trust in me, but also because I'd already made my suspicion known to other people. News travels. "I think he's the one responsible for your injury," I said.

"Was he now? Good riddance then, I say."

"Maybe somebody else thought so himself. Your cousin is with the police department. Can you get him to spill anything useful?"

She tapped her nose. "Leave it to me." Cleo weaved around Jolene's legs, while Adriana hopped onto the table and made the lights flicker. I glared at her. Luckily, Jolene didn't notice anything odd. She typed a quick message on her phone.

"You'll be discreet?"

"Oh, honey," she chuckled. "Hank wouldn't notice subtle if it jumped up and gave him a big old kiss. He won't think twice about me talking about the gosh darn biggest thing that happened since he got his badge. Or else I'll sweet-talk his partner. Tilda Ramos is a great gal."

The name rang a bell. Officer Ramos had been part of the duo that showed up after the break-in, the one I'd nicknamed Marple. That meant Jolene's cousin had to be the one I dubbed Holmes.

"I believe I met them," I said. "What was your cousin's name again?"

"Hank Newby. If I'm lucky, I'll catch him during his lunch break."

She promised to be back after dinner. I had done all I could. Now we just had to wait.

Patience wasn't my strong suit, and Adriana was no better.

To pass the hours, she took me on a sightseeing tour through her old haunts. Cobblewood Cove had grown in the last century, but it hadn't really changed that much, although some of the yards earned Adriana's contempt.

She'd been used to gardeners and manicured lawns. Now there were plastic ornaments and garden gnomes in a handful of places.

The cars also didn't quite measure up, aesthetically. "They all look like boxes," she complained, as we strolled past Fords and Chevrolets and Toyotas. "You should have seen Tommy's automobile. He wouldn't have been seen dead in a jalopy like these things."

I flinched at her innocent remark.

She prattled on. "It was yellow, with green upholstery that matched Belle's eyes, Tommy said. Flash, but not too flash, he said when he chose it. His dad had his heart set on a Bugatti but Tommy wouldn't hear of it. His car could go 80 miles an hour. Just imagine!"

"That must have been pretty expensive," I said. "Didn't you tell me Tommy didn't want anything to do with his father's shady deals?"

"He earned every penny himself. Something to do with engineering, I think." Her voice became vague. "Anyway, he loved that car almost as much as my sister. You could pile in half a dozen suitcases as well."

A loud woof ended our trip down memory lane. Groucho, the dachshund, strained on his leash to greet us.

True to her word, Jolene returned in the evening. Her broad grin made my heart skip a bit. She had something for me. And someone. She'd brought Matt along.

"Sorry I didn't ask," she apologized. "He insisted on driving me."

With good reason, I thought, when I noticed how awkwardly she held her injured hand. Since she would already have told him everything, it didn't matter anyway.

I welcomed them inside and made sure to place Matt next to Jolene.

Adriana could gaze soulfully into his eyes, but that was less distracting than her other antics.

Or she stood still so completely under Cary Grant's spell that her flirting took no other form. I didn't hold my breath though, because I'd poured Jolene a medicinal brandy and my great-great-aunt already sniffed the air with abandon.

Matt declined and stuck to coffee.

I joined him.

"You've got a good nose for crime," Jolene said after she'd sipped her drink and her body relaxed.

"Bert was murdered?"

"Hold your horses," Matt told her. "That much isn't clear yet."

"Baloney," Adriana whispered in the same heartbeat that Jolene said, "Yeah, right, and the pope's getting married in the morning. Of course somebody offed him."

"What exactly did your cousin say?"

She counted the facts on the fingers of her good hand. "No skid marks on the street so he didn't brake hard. Alcohol in his blood stream. A loose wheel that could have made him come off the road."

My disappointment must have shown in my face, because she added, "It's not hard evidence, but it's still a bit much, right? That he'd be so drunk he wouldn't try to brake, and that it just so happened that the wheel came loose? Breaking his neck, too, in the crash. If you ask me, the killer staged an accident. Get the poor dude to pass out, finish him off, and send the car into the ditch."

Adriana grabbed my hand. I felt it as well as I saw it. I gave hers a light squeeze back. The description had sounded nasty, and too plausible to be wrong.

"I'm impressed," I said. "I'd thought post mortem and things would take ages."

"They do, unless the mother of the big boss goes around talking about foul play and incompetent police." I remembered the women I'd overheard. That would explain it.

"Did the dead man have a police record?" I asked.

Jolene pulled a face. "They're not sure yet about his name. The car was still registered to a used car dealer who went out of business a while back."

"What about fingerprints? Or are they waiting for results?"

"I have no idea," she admitted. "But I'll ask Hank." She pulled out her phone.

"If he had that much alcohol in his blood, where would he have been drinking?" I asked. "Maybe there's witnesses who saw him, alone or in company."

"Why are you so interested?" Matt gave me a curious little smile.

"Because he broke in here, and stole her family documents, right?" Jolene grew excited. "Maybe he was after a treasure map. Lots of tales around about folks who hid gold and jewels during the Great Depression. Or money."

Matt rolled his eyes at her. "You've read too much pulp fiction."

"She's right," Adriana told me. "My great-grandmother buried her silver teapot during the civil war, and it took her a whole month to find it again." She eyed Matt with a sudden coldness.

"Too bad he made off with all the important papers from the era when the Darlings had real money." I gave a little titter.

"We're broke?" Adriana gaped at me.

I signaled her, no, wishing she had a shin or ankle I could kick as a warning.

Jolene wrinkled her brow. "But if he'd already stolen what he came for, then why would he return and pose as a handyman?"

That was a very good question, and the one that kept me up at night. Whatever it was Bert had been searching for could still be in the house, and I was as clueless as before what form it took.

If it was a gold coin or several of them, they could be hidden in every nook and cranny, apart from the old servants quarters. Paper could be anywhere.

"All these new locks and bolts should keep him out," I said with as much conviction as I could muster. "If there's anything left that he was after, it's probably now in the museum storeroom. I've taken everything of possible interest to the Schuylers."

"The alarm there is connected to the police station," Matt said. "I've made sure of that. The question is, does our man have any idea this house no longer holds anything of interest?"

"Now you sound like one of my favorite novels," Jolene teased him. "Talking about our man. First you don't believe me and now you're muscling in on our case?"

"Thanks to my job, I have a bit more experience with criminals than you ladies." His face clouded over. "This is not good."

"Fiddlesticks," Jolene said. "Give me until noon, and all the town will know that Genie has given away everything."

I agreed with her. Long live the local gossip. One more night, and we should be as safe as we could possibly be.

Matt's gaze traveled around. "I don't intend to insult you, but from what I've seen, your family was comfortably off, but nothing like the Schuylers and the Harewoods, or even the Wards."

"If it's just a treasure map, it doesn't have to be Genie's family wealth," Jolene pointed out. "In the old days, people would constantly write to each other, or have treasure hunts with clues."

She winked at me. I leant back, suddenly feeling optimistic. I'd picked another smart ally.

My new partner-in-crime poked her chauffeur. "Come on, sunshine. We've got a few things to do before you can have your beauty sleep." Jolene caught my puzzled glance. "It was your idea to put our feelers out in the bars."

He gave in with good grace. "Just promise me, that you'll call, if you hear so much as a leaf rustle outside, okay?"

I gave him a thumbs-up. I'd already worked out how to wedge chair under the handle in my bedroom. Tonight, I'd barricade myself, together with ghost and cat.

CHAPTER TWENTY

"This is a drip," Adriana complained for the umpteenth time, in what I'd identified as the spectral equivalent of kids' "Are we there yet?" and equally grating.

Since Jolene and Matt had left, we'd played card games and I'd read her stories from her *Black Mask* magazine until my voice took on a hitherto unknown husky timbre.

"How about sleep?" I suggested. I might as well have saved my breath.

She gave me a wounded look intent at tugging at my heartstrings. "That's easy for you to say. I'll be up all night, sitting and waiting, sitting and waiting, while you're snoozing." She twiddled her thumbs.

"As long as you don't wake me without a good reason." I yawned wide enough to make my jaw ache and headed to my bed where I buried my face in the pillow. Adriana had shown herself immune to more subtle hints.

Cleo was a lot smarter than me. She'd already drifted off into dreamland, under my bed.

A tragic sigh close to my ears made me bury my face even deeper. Silence fell. Slowly I moved my head until I could spot Adriana out of the corner of my eye. She'd draped herself over an armchair and played with her bangle.

The doorbell ruptured my sleep. I glanced out of the window.

Jolene waved up at me. Nearly ten o'clock. I wrapped myself into my bathrobe and ran downstairs.

Adriana hummed to herself as I apologized for my lack of proper dressing to Jolene.

My delightful ancestor probably felt extraordinarily pleased with herself, to see me twist myself into a verbal pretzel, because I made her let me sleep in.

"No need to say anything," Jolene said. "I just thought you'd want to hear the latest straight from the horse's mouth."

She waited with her revelations until I had enough caffeine in my system to be fully awake.

"Are you sitting down?" She paused after her rhetorical question.

"This is going to be good," Adriana said.

It was.

Bert, or rather Theodore Johnson as his name turned out to be, had been arrested for suspected robbery and for burglary twice. Each time he walked free, without so much as a trial, because the charges had been dropped. "That takes an expensive lawyer," Jolene said. "Or . . ." She gave me an encouraging look.

"Or someone pulled a few strings. Do you have any information about what he'd supposedly stolen?"

"Only that it was private homes he targeted," she said. "You can count yourself lucky my cousin dug up that much."

"Fair enough. But if there's a name or address for Bert's legal counsel, maybe that'll lead us to his last employer."

She shook her head. "Not possible to get hold of that kind of information."

"What about drinking buddies the night of his death?"

"That's the other interesting thing. Matt and I went to every bar within ten miles of the city limits. No-one had seen a stranger."

"Then our killer has made his first mistake," I said.

She frowned. "How so?"

"Unless the police found a bottle of booze in his car. Otherwise, if he didn't visit a bar, where did he manage to get so much alcohol into his blood stream he didn't react at all?"

"He could have throw it in a bin," Jolene said.

"In his state?"

"You're right." She pulled a face as she prepared to leave. "Duty calls, I'm afraid. A new alarm system for the Harewood mansion. That's the third job like this since you had your unwanted visitor, if I count you."

"Does your cousin now believe me, or is he still convinced of his bored teenager story?"

"Hank's keeping an open mind."

She was halfway out the door, when I asked, "Who was the other customer?"

"Fred Ward. Although I have no idea what he thinks is worth shelling out a grand or two for to protect it."

"She's right," Adriana said when we were alone again. "The Wards aren't rolling in dough. Unless the old man has made a lot more from bribes than my dad knew."

"Or later generations made money." Although Fred hadn't a rich man's air. "Of course there's also one more possibility. What if he has discovered something in the library or his family papers that needs protecting at any cost?"

Adriana grew so excited, she floated in the air again. Maybe being a ghost wasn't so bad, I mused. If I should leave this earthly realm and instead be able to talk to the animals and lift off whenever the mood took me, I'd sign up.

My great-great-aunt burst my bubble. "Eek," she said with a decided pinch of her nostrils. "This is too disgusting."

I didn't see or smell anything.

"I know we've somehow become penny-pinching beggars, but honestly?" She pointed an accusing finger at the floorboards where dust had accumulated in the gaps.

"First of all, we're far from beggars," I set the record straight. "Second of all, that's nothing out of the ordinary. If you have feet, you track in some dirt. If you have skin, you shed some cells which settle down as dust. Think of it as traces of your past."

She gave a dramatic shudder. "The Harewoods had three house-maids and a scullery maid to see to those things, and so did the Schuylers. Three! Even our few servants kept the place fresh as a Primrose."

"Well, there are no servants now."

"The Schuylers have a butler," she corrected me. "And I'd bet dollars to donuts that Jonathan and Fred and my darling Matt have someone to take care of them."

"These days, that's usually called a wife, if you go in for old-fashioned," I said.

Her look showed incomprehension. I really should introduce her to modern times and basic feminist ideas. Then again, why spoil her fun, as long as she didn't demand I scrub the floor on my knees, dressed in sacking and with bar soap and a brush?

"How wealthy were you?" I asked. Not that I believed in a treasure map, but if there were a few more jewels to be recovered, they might add to Adriana's substance in every sense of the word.

Okay, I wouldn't say no to a cash injection to my sickly bank account either. I wasn't exactly starving, but Cartier and Dior could sleep well without having to worry about my competition. Being studio-less also meant no new merchandise for a while.

"It's crass for a young lady to talk about money," she said in such a sanctimonious tone that made it clear she was imitating someone.

"Did your dad say that?"

"Grandpa. He said, you can be as rich as Croesus and still be poor in character."

"Ouch. Anyone in particular?"

She gave me her most impressive eye-roll yet. "Why do you think Belle and Tommy had to keep everything hush-hush?"

"That's not very fair on your sister and her boyfriend."

"I told you."

I wondered if the family regretted their harsh judgment that must have spoilt Belle's enjoyment in her last months. I hoped so.

Until lately, I'd considered my forebears as pretty decent, some-times even dashing. The Dueling Darling had been followed a few generations later by the Daredevil Darling, when Adriana's mother had joined a suffragette sister on a risky flight in a monoplane. It was hard to see a woman like that letting the men in her family come down like a ton of bricks on her daughter's boyfriend, because his dad wasn't up to snuff.

"Mommy and he had a blazing row about that," Adriana said, rehabilitating my view of the Daredevil. "But with granddad being sickly..." She dropped the two inches down to the ground and stood on the exact spot she'd complained about.

"He played the invalid card." Really, the tyranny of some people.

"Mommy would have talked him around, and Daddy too. They always gave in to her after a bit of bluster."

"Do you remember seeing any of your mom's stuff?" They'd had a strong connection. If we couldn't track more of Adriana's belongings, maybe other things with a personal connection worked as well. "Did she have any special gems? Or did you have anything?"

A gleam came into her eyes. "She had the sweetest tiara, I remember. She'd wear that to be photographed with the suffragettes, so people could see that they weren't some grubby rabble-rousers. It was all silver and like fine lacy. Belle and I had matching gold lockets, with each other's pictures, and of course there's my necklace." She fell silent.

I hoped the memories hadn't made her too sad.

I worried unnecessarily. Adriana had used her period of contemplation to have a bright idea which I should have come up with.

The museum offered the astonishing amount of two opening hours a week. I suspected that had more to do with a lack of interest from the public and less with the difficulty of enlisting volunteers, especially in a place where most people had deep roots and a surplus of leisure, thanks to their advanced age. Cobblewood Grove had one single primary school and one high school, and that had been unchanged since I could remember.

"I've never been inside the place," Adriana confided as we planned our approach.

I was pretty sure I could have arranged for a private tour of the museum with Dahlia and Primrose. Then again I was also pretty sure Adriana and I would do a lot better unsupervised, especially since my companion still needed to work on the concept of not butting in every minute and making me look like a weirdo.

We were in luck. At four o'clock, the doors would open. Two hours should be ample to have a proper inspection of everything on display. After all, how many objects could there be, without the items kept aside for the great exhibition?

The answer was, a lot. Since the museum's founding days in the early 20th century, generations of civil-minded inhabitants had donated to the collections. At first glance I'd suspected that some of them had also used the opportunity for a little light decluttering to rid themselves of unwanted gifts heirlooms, without treading on toes. A second glance did nothing to make me change my mind on that.

"What a pile of crock," Adriana decided in the first of four rooms. Shelves and cabinets were dedicated to luggage from a tricorn hat box belonging originally to one of Cobblewood Cove's founding fathers to wicker boxes and canvas covered trunks. The Smithsonian wouldn't come running for them anytime soon.

Adriana sniffed the air like a hound on a hot trail. She beckoned me to move on, to the next room.

Five pairs of sightless eyes stared at me. The pupils had been painted blue and brown, to make them life-like. Considering they were made of wood, like the rest of the mannequins, they had an eery effect.

Adriana went straight through the red rope surrounding the life-sized dolls and grasped for the fur trimmed coat one of them wore. It covered an ankle length skirt and a silk blouse in glaring shades of pink. She did manage a slight tug on the sleeve.

"Yours," I concluded with a sense of satisfaction.

She glared daggers at the display. "This is so awful. They've used my best winter coat, and then they put it together with something a chorus girl wouldn't put on."

Her sartorial sense was so offended she barely reacted when some-one else entered the room.

I made up for it by almost jumping out of my skin when someone touched my shoulder.

"Jonathan." I shaded my eyes with my hand to cover up a nervous twitch. My nerves had suffered a lot in a few days. "Don't tell me you're volunteering here?"

His smile crinkled his eyes in a way that made Adriana leave the mannequin alone and plant herself in front of him. A flirty expression spread over her face.

161

"Heavens, no," he said. "To be honest, I saw you going in."

"Oh."

"Someone's carrying a torch for you," Adriana whispered in my ear.

A warm, fuzzy feeling spread in my stomach. A woman does like to know she's appreciated, and that had been something I'd missed out on for over a year.

My last serious relationship had been a while ago. Not that I was considering anything of that sort, I hastened to add to myself. It simply felt good to have someone sophisticated and attractive show interest in my company.

Jonathan copied the pose of one of the mannequins in male clothing. In its hand, the doll held a walking stick, and a silk top hat sat on its head. A bushy fake moustache and large sideburns fit in with the description on a card that gave the manufacturing year of the attire as 1905.

I looked closer. The name of the original wearer was omitted. The donors on the other hand were named as the Ward family. One of the mayors had originally owned this finery, I guessed.

Jonathan pointed out another ensemble, which could have been worn by Queen Victoria. "One of ours, I'm afraid. We had a certain liking for showing off our wealth."

"Not all of you though," I said, remembering what I'd heard about Tommy.

"I hope so." He chuckled. "Is there anything in particular you're interested in? I could show you around. Save you the tedium of going through every single thing here."

I repeated my pretext of searching for design inspiration.

"You've come to the wrong place," he said. "The good stuff will be with its rightful owners. I can have a hunt around in the Harewood collection, if you want me to." He gave me a shrewd glance. "Dahlia and Primrose will vouch for my respectability, if you've got qualms to see me alone in my home. Or I could bring the things to your place. I was going to see if you need my assistance anyway with carrying or whatever else you're doing to get rid of old junk."

Adriana's head bobbed up and down in a vigorous nod.

"After dinner okay for you?" His phone pinged. He grimaced. "I've got to run. See you then, Genie." He scanned the display once more as he headed for the door. "Beats me why they'd beef up security in every room. As if anyone would want to steal these things."

Adriana's face lit up like a Christmas display. I covered my ears. Too late. As I'd feared, my great-great-aunt said, "Let's do it."

"We can't."

She stomped her foot and tugged again at the sleeve. "It's not stealing when it's mine."

We entered a staring contest. I held my own for about 30 seconds. "I'll think of something," I said.

"I know you will." She pulled me along. "Come on, there might be more loot."

CHAPTER TWENTY-ONE

T he museum contained two more items Adriana simply had to have, as she declared. One was a pair of flying goggles that would have done Amelia Earhart proud. They'd belonged to the Daredevil Darling, Rosalind.

I agreed with her. It beggared belief that anyone would have parted with that kind of treasure, yet kept the chamber pots I'd offloaded onto the Schuylers.

The second item held less historic value, but Adriana insisted the hatpin used to be hers and technically still was.

The only snag I saw was how to claim them back without having to resort to breaking and entering, which thanks to Matt's meddling would have been impossible for me. And the only burglar I knew was dead as a doornail, not that I'd have hired him.

"We could do a deal," I suggested when we were home. We - or rather I as in the only one having a useful body - were sifting through the house once again.

I'd decided to move everything remotely connected to letters, documents and photographs, to my cavernous wardrobe. If Jonathan put in his promised appearance or anyone else dropped by, like Matt for example, or Jolene, it would ruin my story that there was nothing left to see here.

I carefully wrapped albums and bundled letters in a towel and stowed them away in a suitcase. Their perusal was still on my to-do list, once I had the leisure to read through a ton of pages written in spidery pen strokes. Adriana had opted out of that task. Her eyes weren't up to it, she declared. I decided to leave it at that.

A stack of clothes covered the divan in the drawing room when I declared the job finished. Adriana had decided they were all too dreary for words, so they could all be offered to Dahlia and Primrose in exchange for the safe return of Adriana's belongings.

If none of the bustled skirts and striped suits caught their fancy, I had to come up with another idea. Now though I had more important things to do. Like wash my face and put on some make-up under Adriana's exacting scrutiny.

She had given up on convincing me to pluck my eyebrows into the thin line her era demanded, and feigned horror when she saw my powder-less beauty arsenal.

Apart from that, she approved of my grooming once I'd brushed my hair into obedience and put on some lipstick and mascara. Well, if I say approved . . .

"You'd look prettier in a dress," she said. "You've got nice pins." She stretched a slim leg and admired it.

I ignored her suggestion. My jeans and shirt were good enough for me, and Jonathan didn't mind either, if I interpreted his appreciative manner correctly.

My guest arrived a little late, with a large jewelry case and a bottle of wine in his hands.

He headed straight for Adriana's chair. She giggled and slipped onto the arm, before I steered Jonathan to another seat that had the advantage of being empty. She pouted at me. I stopped myself at the last second from glaring at her, in front of a witness.

"I hope you don't have a sore head today," Jonathan said as he opened the bottle and filled two glasses.

"I've managed to stay accident-free."

We clinked glasses.

The Harewood jewels were a sight to behold. At least two pairs of chandelier earrings had to be genuine diamonds and sapphires by Van Cleef and Arpels, and the bracelets shouted Tiffany to any connoisseur. I barely dared touch them.

"Any good for you?" He sipped his wine as I took out a loupe to study the details.

"Wow. Should you even be carrying the around? They're worth a fortune."

"The insurance thinks so, if I go by the premiums." He seized on my own creations which adorned my earlobes. "You're very talented. You should be selling in every important store in the country."

"Thanks, but you flatter me. I don't see myself working at that level, or cranking out that many quality pieces." I rarely used molds, preferring the uniqueness of each piece I crafted. Also, my sales pitch had been rejected by the houses the likes of him did their shopping at.

He scanned the room and fixed his gaze on the wall which still held Lottie's tapestry. "That's unusual," he said.

"To say the least. I'd have given it to the museum, but it's not vintage."

"Which reminds me, if there's anything I can carry for you?" He jumped up with an athlete's agility.

Adriana shamelessly watched his every move.

"You mentioned the attic," he said.

He might have regretted his chivalry as he inched his way down with a carved tea chest that I'd ignored as too unwieldy for me.

He made it safely to the hallway with it. "Anything else?" he asked. "Maybe that dividing screen? You don't have to come up."

Adriana shook her head.

"This should definitely be enough. The Schuyler sisters will have more than enough to fill a dozen museums if this goes on." I ran my fingers over the 200 year old chest, imagining its perilous journey across the ocean.

"More wine?" He topped up my glass, and only mine.

"You're not drinking any more?"

"I'd take a coffee if you have one."

"Black or cream and sugar?"

"Black." He followed me into the kitchen, with a sheepish expression on his face. "Actually, there's something I wanted to tell you."

I stopped filling water into the machine. "Yes?"

"That man you asked about, the one you think broke into your home?"

I started the coffee machine, keeping my back to Jonathan. "What about him?"

"He had a car accident. I'm afraid Bert is dead."

I clapped my hand in front of my mouth. "How awful. Are you sure?"

"As sure as I can be. One of the officers told me."

"I may sound cruel," I said, "but I don't think I'll lose sleep over him. At least I won't have to worry about him coming back."

"That's the right attitude," he said. "And maybe now your belongings will be recovered."

"Even if not, it's not the end of the world. It would have been different if he'd made off with valuable things, like your family's gems."

That sobering thought put an end to our conversation. Jonathan excused himself soon after. He had a well-honed sense for when a woman needed to be alone with herself and her great-great-aunt.

I stood at the door until Jonathan drove off, with the tea chest on the back seat of his Mercedes.

Adriana watched him too. She'd stayed away from the wine fumes or possibly the coffee had sobered her up. "He really likes you," she said with a wistful undertone.

"I am quite lovable," I quipped.

"I mean it. He went to all that trouble, to chat to the police about that awful goon. They like him too, or they wouldn't have talked to him."

"He's a big deal in this town," I reminded her.

"And those shiners? Imagine bringing them over for you to steal the idea."

"I don't steal. I borrow inspirations."

She snickered. "That's what mommy's friend said when she bought the same hat as Belle. She looked like a hundred year's old in it."

168

Then she cocked her head to the side, deep in thought.

"You know where we haven't searched yet for Mommy's things?"

"The garage. But that's a recent addition." In the 19th century, the Darlings and many other families had their own coach house and a private stable a few streets away. The coachman would bring them around when needed. In Adriana's days, the horses were gone and instead a gleaming Packard stood in the coach house, half a mile away since the original shortcut had been taken up by new homes. A modern garage had been added to the back of the house after the war.

"No, silly. In the safe."

CHAPTER TWENTY-TWO

I could have slapped her, if that had been possible. To think of all the running up and down, shoving around boxes and hitting my shins and head in the process, all because Adriana had neglected to mention such a trifling thing as a safe.

She did have the decency to act contrite when I told her in very clear terms what I thought of that.

"I'd forgotten." Her voice sounded tiny.

Cleo ran up to her and gave me a swipe with her paw.

Perfect. I'd managed the feat of being in the cat's·dog-house again.

"Do you think there's something wrong with me?" Adriana asked.

A small part of me wanted to say, Apart from the obvious? The nicer part of me instead said, "No way. Now, where is that safe?"

I should have known it would be hidden behind the heaviest tapestry Lottie had ever created, and a painting behind the cross-stitched scene depicting butterflies in a meadow.

The smallest butterfly was the size of my head. It had taken Lottie a while to get the hang of scaling down.

The watercolor deserved better, I judged. I took it to be an excellent copy of a Hopper, or at least in the same school.

It had been screwed to the wall so long ago the screws themselves had turned black. It took me several attempts to remove them so I could lift the painting off and lowered it to the ground. Behind sat a ton of black steel, let into the wall.

The Victor Safe and Lock company of Cincinnati would be proud to see its excellent state after more than a century. I on the other hand would have preferred something less imposing.

A keyhole and a key would have been nice. Instead, I had to deal with a complicated looking combination lock, and who knew how many deadbolts inside.

This was a serious safe.

Adriana floated a few inches off the ground again, so pleased was she with her cleverness.

"And now?" I asked.

"We open it. Golly, do you think there's a bundle of dough inside? Daddy always kept emergency funds." She rubbed her hands together.

"Do you remember the combination for the lock?"

"I do, actually." A tiny frown creased her forehead. "At least - it'll come to me. If you stop rushing me."

Cleo bobbed her head at her. Adriana added, "And we could do with a nibble. I haven't had a noseful in ages."

The bacon sizzled in the pan, with Adriana hovering nearby. Both she and Cleo were licking their lips, when she exclaimed, "The Christmas ball."

I waited for her to elucidate further.

She pointed at the pan.

I hastened to slide the bacon onto a plate and waft it under her nose.

"Heavenly," she said.

Cleo received her share too, and then I waited for Adriana to speak.

"It's when my parents met," she said. "Dad used to call it the happiest day of his life."

"That's sweet. When exactly was this serendipitous meeting? I assume one year in December."

She counted back on her fingers. "1903. On a Saturday night.

"Now we're getting somewhere."

I consulted my phone. The possible dates had been December 5, 12 or 19. Add to that 1903, and we had numbers to play with.

The third attempt worked like a charm. With nary a squeak the heavy door swung open.

Inside, I spotted several velvet boxes and a steel box.

With a dry sensation in my mouth I reached inside.

Even Adriana acknowledged the importance of this moment with awed silence.

Systematically I removed the velvet boxes first and lined them up on the table. The steel box I reserved for last, a little like in my childhood when I'd spoon out the chocolate pudding first until I'd allow myself to enjoy the cream on top.

The first two velvet boxes each contained a pair of long sapphire and diamond earrings. My silversmith's instincts came to the fore. I itched to look at the intricate craftsmanship, and that of the matching bracelets and necklaces we uncovered next.

The last velvet box held the biggest treasure, Adriana's first curl of hair, lovingly preserved in a locket. I could see her colors grow more vivid and her hair shinier as she fastened it around her neck.

I no longer had to avert my gaze because it was too spooky to see the same object on her and in its box. Instead I admired the scenario.

If we kept on at this rate, she'd soon be anchored enough in her past to move further away from me than two or three yards when we left the house. That cheered me up enormously.

As much as I'd come to appreciate her company, there were things I preferred to do alone. Like going to the bathroom without a running commentary from outside. However the spirit world worked, it cloaked everything to do with her from everyone and everything but me. Or cats, dogs, and parrots.

"Can you now please stop lollygagging?" she gazed at the steel box. Surprise, surprise, it needed a key, which was still lacking.

"Let me have a peek," she ordered.

I made way for her.

"Duck soup." She did a little shimmy. "Do you have a hairpin?"

I made a quick trip to the dresser downstairs and returned to find her peering inside the keyhole with the concentration of a master-shot taking aim.

I cleared my throat and she jumped up. "You scared me."

"Sorry." I handed her the hairpin or rather, tried.

She didn't bother to move a muscle. "Haven't you ever opened a lock before?"

"Not without permission, no. I've also never been locked up in a dungeon, or a broom cupboard, or sent to languish in my room."

"It's fun. Belle and I used to sneak into the kitchen and help our-selves to sugar cookies."

"I hope your parents didn't blame the maids, or the cook." I knew enough about the perils of servants in the not always good old days.

"Of course not. It was Mommy who taught us this trick."

She made me bend the thin metal a little and go fishing with it inside the keyhole until I felt resistance.

Sweat rolled down my temple as the mechanism inside gave way at last and I could open the lid.

"Money."

Adriana had been right. Her dad had kept a wad of ten and twenty dollar bills in the safe. He'd also stored birth and marriage certificates inside, as well as jewelry boxes with necklaces and the receipts for them.

The large box also contained a note to his wife and daughters, in case anything happened to him. The gems had been intended for his girls' wedding day. He'd purchased them in New York the year before, when Belle returned from Switzerland.

Why exactly all these items were still in the safe, was an intrigu-ing question, but the wrong one for today. More important was the conclusion that we were no further. Richer, yes. The baubles alone would fetch a five figure sum, if Aimée decided against keeping it. But smarter, no. And Aimée's return was alarmingly close.

We had to come up with a new idea, something that was about overdue. I shone a torch inside the safe. Maybe I'd overlooked some-thing. I hadn't.

I kicked the wall, only to hop around because my foot hurt.

"That was stupid," Adriana chided me. "Don't tell me you didn't know that was going to happen."

"It's easy to be wise after the fact." I shut my mouth, dumbstruck. A glimmer of an idea formed in my head. True, it had its weak spots, namely that it relied on normal human reaction, but I was willing to try it, unless something better came to mind.

Which is why my trusty sidekick and I hit the road in the evening to enlist the help we needed to spring a trap.

Chapter Twenty-Three

In the morning, we went over the plan again. I'd mapped it out, down to the last detail I could think of. A lot depended on the availability of people and the speed of rumors. Usually they spread like wildfire. Today, I planned on doing my hardest to ensure that.

The first stop on our bait and wait tour of Cobblewood Cove took me within dangerously close reach of Miss Lola's ever ready scissors.

"Do you all know Genie Darling, Amy's little girl?" She asked the three ladies under the hairdryers. Miss Lola had to raise her voice over the electric hum, but since everyone gave her a thumbs up, I would have given them full marks for their hearing. Unless simply agreeing was the easiest response to Miss Lola's questions.

"Now, what can I do for you?"

"I was wondering . . ."

A fanatic gleam came into her eyes as she fastened her gaze on my locks.

"Sit." She made cutting motions. "You've got split ends."

I cleared my throat.

"Do what she says," Adriana ordered. "What's the worst that can happen?"

Meekly, I followed Miss Lola to the sink.

"That's better," she said, as she shampooed and rinsed with abandon before she led me to a chair.

Adriana meanwhile ran her hands over her own impeccable coiffure. The traitor. She also treated me to all of her thoughts on the salon decorations, which tended towards pink and glossy, and the pictures of classic movie stars, which tended towards Doris Day and Elizabeth Taylor.

"You could do with a different style," Adriana said. "Something exciting that'll make all your admirers go crazy."

I gritted my teeth.

"Think of it. Do you plan to end up a sad, old spinster like the tapestry woman?"

She'd gone too far. I sat up bolt upright and told her in no uncertain way, "Yes."

Unfortunately I'd been so focused on Adriana that I'd paid no attention to what Miss Lola had said to me simultaneously.

To my horror, the scissors snipped, and a lock of my hair fell to the floor. She'd taken my yes for an agreement to go all out with my hair.

"Now, what is it you wanted to talk about, Genie?" She took a step back to check for straggling hairs. I blinked through the first bangs I'd sported since my pre-teens.

"How about a tint?" One of the ladies under a dryer cackled. "Lola's a dab hand with color."

"That's true, even if I say it myself. Ask the younger Miss Schuyler. You wouldn't know she's not a natural blonde if you saw her, now would you?"

"Amazing." I stifled a whimper. "But not for me, thank you. All I really wanted was to ask you if you could recommend anyone who could help me open an old safe. I've found one hidden in the villa."

Three heads popped out from under the dryers, revealing three sets of hearing aids. That accounted for their swift reaction.

"A secret safe?" Miss Lola leant closer. "Oh, my."

"It is exciting," I admitted. "I only wish I could open it."

Four sets of eyes bulged with curiosity. The ladies itched to leave their chairs and chew over this delicious morsel with their friends.

"I'll have to think about it," Miss Lola said. "I'll call you as soon as I come up with a name. Now, how about we add a little height to your new do?"

I could feel my eyeballs skitter back as she grabbed the teasing comb.

"Why are you so sore?" Adriana asked as we left the premises.

I ignored her question.

"Genie, Genie, Genie," she hummed in my ear.

"Fine." I fumbled in my earbuds, so at least I could pretend I was chatting to a real person.

"I'm waiting."

"Take a good look at what you've done," I hissed.

"Me?"

178

I tugged at my teased locks.

"You. Because of your badgering, Miss Lola turned me into the spitting image of Rose in Golden Girls."

Adriana stared at me, uncomprehending.

I gave up explaining.

Dahlia and Primrose welcomed me with compliments about my hair, and open arms. As much as it pained me to keep silent, I bit my tongue and decided I'd just have to wear a hat until Christmas or so.

It would have been the wrong move to squander their good will which the correct diagnosis of parrot Petey had gained me.

"Tell them a sob story," Adriana said. She'd picked up that expression on the street, together with others I'd struggled to explain without entangling myself in explanations.

Heck, I was barely in my thirties and I had trouble keeping up with teenagers and acronyms.

"I have a huge favor to ask," I said as we sat down for homemade lemonade and chocolate chip cookies.

The picture was as wholesome as can be, if one omitted the fact that I sported the hairstyle from hell, had come on a mission of deceit and treachery, and someone else in this stately mansion was most likely a mastermind of crime.

I corrected myself.

A mastermind wouldn't have sent someone like Bert slash Theodore to do his dirty work.

A tiny voice in my head reminded me of my unwitting complicity in his death. I shut it down and concentrated on the task at hand.

"It's my mother," I said.

The sisters were all sympathetic ear. "Is anything the matter with her?"

"Heavens, no." I added a little trill, to show just how peachy everything was with her. "It's only - when I told her that you, or rather the museum, have in your possession the most important items in the history of the Darling family, she almost--"

"Fainted?" Adriana suggested. "Broke into a song and dance?"

"She was so excited. These links to our proudest days mean so much to her. Of course I wouldn't dream to ask you to simply hand over the flying goggles and the fur coat which Adriana Darling wore when she met John Gilbert. I can replace them with other objects that are just as valuable to the museum, but without that sentimental value for us." A slight wobble in my voice emphasized my story."

"John Gilbert? How wonderful." The sisters interest grew. "George told us the goggles could be quite valuable, but wait until we tell him about the coat."

"George?"

"He hates to brag," Dahlia said. "We trust you not to tell anyone, Genie, but really he has taken on the most hands-on approach to our little project. He spent hours looking at every single item."

"How kind," I said, silently gritting my teeth. He'd been searching for whatever Bert had been after.

Dahlia turned to her sister. "If we made up a sign about John Gilbert and Miss Darling, that would be a coup for the local press."

"We should give them a heads-up," Primrose said. "Maybe we can rouse national interest."

I couldn't believe my ears. How could they ignore my heartfelt request?

"It was only a brief encounter," I said. "He waved at Adriana outside a theatre, that's all."

"Still, John Gilbert." Dahlia clutched her heart. "That must have been something."

"Which is why my mother really wants the coat and the goggles back."

"We understand," Primrose said. "And you shall have them, as soon as the exhibit closes in three months."

Adriana shot off her seat. "Mean old trouts."

Dahlia rubbed her thin arms. "Did you feel that sudden draft?"

I shook my head in denial as Primrose reached for a thin cape. Adriana moved closer to the sisters, and they shivered. I signaled her to stop. We had one last message to deliver.

I did it on the way out. "It's such a pity that I can't open the secret safe," I said. "Who knows what's inside, but these craftsmen did incredible work, if you consider the piece dates back to the early 20th century."

Curiosity masked as historic interest propelled them closer. "We never knew about a safe."

"Neither did I, or my mother, until I stumbled upon it. Never mind, I'll ask the Head Librarian for assistance. She told me she can find out just about anything under the sun, if Miss Lola can't provide me with the name of a craftsman."

To add a veneer of truth to that lie, I made sure a few townspeople saw me make my way to Daphne's desk. I had to bypass Fred, which caused me a little pang of regret, until I remembered that I hadn't fully cleared him of any duplicity.

Daphne showed the correct amount of interest in the idea of a hidden safe, a missing combination, and using her skills to find the needed sesame or whatever magic words librarian used to describe this sort of situation. She offered to pop around as soon as she had the goods, but settled for an invitation for tomorrow night. By then, I fully intended to have tranquility restored in the Darling abode, and any danger averted.

Adriana whizzed around, blissfully unaware that our adventure together might come to an end. I had a few hours left before I had to have everything in place, including our last defense. It was only fair to leave the planning for this short window to my great-great-aunt.

Maybe she sensed it too. I'd expected her to opt for the Cocoa Cabana with its tantalizing smells, or a movie session with back-to-back Cary Grant movies (I wasn't totally averse to that idea), but she surprised me.

Her face took on one of her rare wistful expressions. "I'd like to see my parents, and my sister."

This stopped me in my tracks. "Meet, as in - you said you're the only one of your kind around." We'd decided to omit the g-word. It didn't do her justice. Also, she blew out the fuses whenever she heard it.

182

"I want to see their graves."

Cobblewood Cove's cemetery had once been in a remote location at the edge of town. Nowadays, two small housing estates with pastel colored bungalows flanked the park-like setting with its shaded avenue.

A marble headstone marked the final resting place of Daredevil Rosalind and her husband. Adriana hugged it. "I'm so sorry for everything," she whispered.

I gave her some space, or as much as she could physically take. Or was it non-physically?

When she had composed herself, I led her to her own grave where her body had been interred next to her sisters since 1929. She read the inscription on the headstone, and her head swiveled around so fast I had to close my eyes.

"That's all wrong? Why isn't she old? She should have been ancient when she passed away. And where is he?" Adriana asked.

"Who?"

"Her husband. Tommy Harewood."

I had to sit down. There was no bench close by, and planting my behind on the headstone would have been too disrespectful, so I sank onto the grass. "Her husband?"

She tugged on my sleeve. "I want to see him. And could you please tell me what's going on here?"

There was no easy way to tell her. "I'm so sorry. They were in a car crash. Tommy was killed on the spot. Belle fought hard, but she passed away a few days later.

Adriana broke out into heart-wrenching sobs. I hated to interrupt her, except I had no choice. We needed to hurry home. For now I knew everything.

Chapter Twenty-Four

"When did Belle get married and why didn't I read about it in the newspaper?"

I rattled the bolted windows. They held fast. Ditto the front door. Good, I couldn't afford to leave a second line of attack. When our pigeon came, it had to be through the back door.

Adriana had tears running down her cheeks. "It was a secret. Daddy had been so shirty about Tommy's crooked old man that Belle wanted him to simmer down. Also it would have caused a lot of talk, with Tommy's old man barely cold in his grave."

That made sense.

Her voice quivered. "That night when I fell into the water, we'd come back from celebrating their wedding. I'd been their bridesmaid and witness, together with a clerk at the registry."

"That explains why the marriage certificate isn't in the safe. Either Belle or Tommy must have kept it."

"It would have been Belle. She used to help Daddy with his paperwork. He'd have been lost without her."

"Where would she have filed it away?"

"I'll show you."

Cleo used her claws to scratch on a floorboard in Belle's former room. I sat her aside and got to work. Underneath the floor I found a hidey-hole similar to the one in the nursery. "My notebook," Adriana cried out.

Inside, a dried rose served as a bookmark. Belle had added a note, listing all the poems and stories she'd read to Adriana while she hoped against hope for her sister's recovery.

A lump in my throat made it hard to swallow. Married or not, the sisters belonged together. Here was the heartfelt proof of their bond.

The certificate of marriage was in a large, official manila envelope, together with Tommy's letters to Belle in Switzerland. I refrained from reading them, or doing anything else. That decision was up to Adriana.

I put everything back except for the envelope. I had plans for it.

Night took forever to fall. For a town as small as this, there was a hard to believe amount of traffic, and of people strolling past on the sidewalk. My nerves were taut as violin strings and as easy to snap when finally, all went silent.

I'd taken down the tapestry and cleared the way between the vintage wall safe and the equally vintage wardrobe that took up the wall opposite. I'd drilled a couple of small holes into the walnut doors. Now all I could do was wait for our trap to be sprung.

Cleo stood watch with Adriana and me, still as a statue and as imposing as her ancestor Bastet which had been revered as divine.

I'd tied a thin thread with the bell I'd removed from Cleo's collar when she moved in with me, around the handle of the back door. It would warn us of an intruder without alerting him.

The thread slipped off, the bell hit the floor with a tiny jingle, and Adriana and I hid behind the sofa in the room with the safe.

A finger of light danced around as our man used a torch to find his way around. He crept up to the safe.

I switched on the lights. "I assume you want this?" I held up the manila envelope.

He shielded his eyes against the sudden brightness. The charming facade had worn off like the gold plating on a cheap ring. Instead, Jonathan Harewood looked fit to commit murder.

Again.

He lunged forward.

I took a step back. "Is this really worth killing for?"

"Keeping a fortune?" He lunged again. "Have a guess."

For the second time, I dodged him, just barely.

Adriana had to be somewhere behind me. I was only dimly aware of that. I had other worries.

Jonathan had surprised me.

Stupid, stupid, stupid, a small voice in my head went. I'd relied too much on all these arranged accidents to have considered him using a gun.

I was wrong.

The small pistol in his hand had a dull shine that matched the flatness of his pupils. How I could ever have thought him attractive, eluded me. In this light, he had the menacing air of the thug he was underneath the expensive clothing and cultured veneer.

My voice came out in a rasp. "Did you have this all planned? Get rid of Bert, and then murder me?"

He fixed me with an unblinking gaze. "You're about to die and yet you wonder about an unimportant man? You're really a breath of fresh air, Genie. Or rather, were."

"Enlighten me. Instead of a cigarette and a hearty last meal?"

A soft chuckle rewarded me. I prayed that his vanity would keep him talking and me alive.

"It's his own fault. If he'd done his job well, you wouldn't have been able to suspect him, or anyone."

"That's true," I admitted. "Without his botched burglary I wouldn't have dreamt of thinking there'd be anything of importance hidden away. But why did you wait so long? The house sat empty for weeks."

"Because, Genie dearest, just like you I had no idea, until I went through old family stuff for this silly exhibition. Lo and behold, there it was, black on white in a diary, that Thomas Harewood intended to make a match with his girlfriend."

"The cousin," I said. "Your great-great-grandfather, I assume? He manipulated Tommy's car to kill him and Belle Darling."

"He'd only intended to get rid of Tommy," he corrected me. "The moron intended to cut all the profitable business ties and - wait for it - become Mr Charity. I mean, honestly, who in their right mind would allow that to happen?"

"You knew, of course."

"My granddad told me on his deathbed. It's a proud bit of family history, if you look at it from the right perspective. A young man who made his fortune with one bold move."

"His murder method was a little more refined than yours." My heart beat loud in my ears. "There are a few doubts about Bert's death."

"Nothing to do with me." He waved the pistol around. "Just like there's nothing to connect me to the fire in your house. I rather think you tried to open the safe with a small flame cutter and set the room on fire. Smoke inhalation is so dangerous."

He shrugged off a backpack while pointing the gun now straight at my heart.

"Now, if you don't mind, hand me that envelope."

I stepped out from behind the sofa. My teeth chattered with fear. If I had miscalculated, I'd find out soon enough if coming back as a ghost was an option.

"Duck," Adriana yelled. The lights went out, she hissed "Booh," and I dived behind the sofa.

Jonathan swore over the sound of a wardrobe opening. Then came the blessed beam of a small flashlight and a loud thud.

The ceiling lights went on again.

Jonathan lay crumbled to the floor.

Jolene had felled him with a baseball bat. "Hold this," she demanded while she cuffed his hands on his back.

"Is he still breathing?" Adriana asked with a tinge of disappointment.

"Do you have everything on record?" I asked Jolene.

She arched her eyebrows at me. "I've even used a second phone as a back-up. If I do a job, I do it right."

Officers Newby and Ramos picked up Jonathan. He'd have a lot of explaining to do once he left the prison infirmary.

"What was this all about?" Jolene asked once we were done with our statements, and she'd taken me home.

"Money. If my family could prove that Belle Darling had been rightfully married to Thomas Harewood, she, and after her, her closest family, had stood to inherit his fortune. She survived her husband, so the cousin and later down the line, Jonathan would have gone empty-handed. He even stuck to the old family murder recipe."

"Not very original, then."

"No. Thankfully."

My head throbbed.

Cleo jumped onto my lap, after looking to Adriana for permission.

"I'll see myself out," Jolene said. "You look like death warmed up. And I'm not even asking what you've done to your hair."

I bolted the door after her and swallowed a couple of painkillers. "Show me the Black Bottom again," I heard myself saying. "I'm sure I'll be able to wrap my head around it."

"It's not your head that's the problem. It's your feet." Adriana sprang into action when I started our playlist.

I followed suit, and managed to tie myself into a knot even worse than usual. Still, I danced on until my feet hurt and I settled down with my great-great-aunt and the cat to wait for the inevitable, now that we'd solved the case.

CHAPTER TWENTY-FIVE

O ne needed acrobatic skills to overcome the mountains of quilts and tapestries in two of the rooms when the honeymooners made their grand entrance. The rest of the house sparkled after an incredible amount of elbow-grease and helpful little commentaries from Adriana who must have been a nightmare for the maids if she'd used the same zeal in her youth.

I'd put fresh flowers in a dozen vases, a stitched welcome banner hung over the doorway to the honeymoon suite, courtesy of Lottie, and Adriana had waited by my window since the crack of dawn. I knew that first-hand because she'd kept me informed about any single movement outside.

I'd resigned myself to puffy eyes. They were a small price to pay for someone who'd saved my life or at least played a big part in a happy ending for us and jail for Jonathan.

I also wasn't sure how long our partnership would last. Adriana didn't know, but I was certain that her missing necklace held the key to her own death. I'd read every single scrap in the old newspapers. Nobody had found the piece of jewelry, after Adriana had fallen into the water. Considering it would have been worth a handsome sum even back then, whoever pushed her must have grabbed it.

Jonathan's ancestor wouldn't have dared to, but then he must have hired help. If my theory was correct, the necklace might still turn up somewhere and lead me to the person ultimately responsible for Adriana's death. Maybe then she could move on and be reunited with her sister.

A lump in my throat made it hard to swallow. In the little time we'd spent together, I'd come to adore my great-great-aunt, unpredictable and quirky as she was.

The doorbell chimed. Jolene had helped me upgrade it from a boring ring to a a a cheerful jingle.

Aimée glowed with happiness as she snuggled into the crook of Tony's elbow. He too shone with satisfaction.

I hugged my mother and then him. It surprised us both. We'd been on great terms during their courtship but I'd never been a natural hugger.

Cobblewood Cove brought out a lot of new traits in me.

"How marvelous this all looks," Aimée said as I led her to her room. "You've worked wonders."

Adriana cleared her throat. She'd hidden behind me because we'd decided it would be best if Aimée had a chance to freshen up and relax before I introduced them.

My mother peered into the mirror to check her make-up.

Her movements were the same as Adriana's. Certain things clearly did run in the family, if they had bypassed me or not.

"In here," she called out to her new husband. He carried in her suitcases with an ease that made me stop from offering my help.

I didn't want to offend his male pride, when he was more than capable of doing the heavy lifting. Also, my arms hurt from the scrubbing and polishing.

"Ahem," Adriana said. Her patience had worn thin.

"Why don't I let you unpack, and then we'll meet in the dining room?" I said. "If Tony gives us ten minutes? I've got a surprise for you."

Aimée could never resist a surprise. Tony shooed us out and winked at me. I hoped he'd be as understanding when he heard about the latest developments in the Darling family.

I'd set out the second best tea set, in case Aimée dropped anything when I introduced Adriana.

Instead, my mother searched the room. "Where is it?"

She passed Adriana without paying her any attention as she continued her search. "Where is my surprise?"

Adriana and I shared a puzzled look.

"You haven't seen anything?"

Cleo came running. "There she is," I exclaimed. "Look what she brought you." I pretended to remove a piece of paper from her collar and handed the note to my mother.

Adriana's shoulders slumped. My mother, her very own flesh and blood, couldn't see her. It was still only the two of us and the cat.

I took Aimée and Tony to the safe. I'd written the combination on the note I'd passed to my mother. "Open it," I said.

"My goodness," she said as she saw the two sets of gems. "To think nobody had any idea. My clever, clever Genie."

"I believe Rosalind and her husband couldn't bring themselves to see these pieces ever again, or to part with them. Too many memories after their daughters died."

Aimée dabbed her eyes. "Now you're making me cry."

"Don't," I said. "There's also a few more things I should mention."

The newlyweds were left speechless as I recounted my adventures, omitting only Adriana's contribution and our four-legged assistants. We had brought the dogs a few treats as a thank-you, but their names would not feature in any reports.

I had little intention to be sent for psychiatric evaluation, which would have been inevitable.

Tony found his speech first. "I'll set my lawyers to work."

"But what if I don't want the money?" Aimée leant her head against his shoulder. "Could you bear the idea that we'd profit from a young couple being murdered in cold blood?"

"You don't have to keep it," Tony said. I nodded in agreement. "We can give the money away. What we're not going to do is let Jonathan Harewood keep it."

Cleo meowed. She and Adriana huddled together.

I wished I could understand what they were talking about. I also wished I could join in. Instead, I gave Aimée and Tony some privacy while they digested all the information.

Adriana marched around and around in circles. "You said she'd see me. You said she'd be another friend. Fine family I have."

"I'm sorry," I said. "You've still got me, and Cleo, although we'll have to share her with my mother."

"And now? They'll hog you and all the space and we won't be able to do anything."

If I hadn't been sure that her despondency rarely lasted longer than a few minutes, I'd have worried about my poor neglected great-great-aunt. As things were, all I had to do was play, "If You Knew Susie Like I Know Susie" and dance the Charleston with her.

Aimée burst into the room halfway through the dance. Adriana glowered, daring me to stop.

I didn't, and my mother beamed so hard at her suddenly nimble, well, nimble-ish, daughter, that I put all my heart into my efforts.

"That was terrific, sweetheart." My mother broke into applause. "How about doing a little number for the grand opening?"

"What?"

Her laughter rang out in a pleasing arpeggio, again reminding me of Adriana. "I promised Dahlia and Primrose to come up with a few ideas to make things a little more exciting. You can't expect people to drop everything for a bit of rope-cutting and a room or two full of old things that were sitting in attics all over town?"

"She's right," Adriana said. "Tell her you'll do a nifty little number if she gets me my coat. I'll teach you. It'll be a breeze."

"No way," I said, a little more forcefully than planned. Aimée shot me a startled look.

"I'm the reason one of Cobblewood Cove's finest is locked up. They'll either hate me for it or badger me for all the details. I don't think I could take that."

I'd already slammed down the phone on two reporters. Lottie had kept a landline going, and I'd forgotten to cancel it. Ignoring the ringtone was out of the question though, because they gave Cleo a headache. At least that's what I was told.

"Of course, I should have realized." Aimée stroked my hand.

Adriana moved closer to me. So did Cleo.

A little chortle escaped me. Three people, all claiming their share of my attention, if you could count a ghost and a cat as people.

"Do you want to stay home?" Aimée's hand was warm and reassuring and made me feel like a child again.

I hesitated. Adriana gave me a wounded look and I felt her presence even stronger. Technically alive or not, she needed me.

"You have two days to decide." Aimée blew me a kiss as she left, to prepare for a picnic at the beach. Eating food with half a pound of sand in it was a family tradition she'd promised to introduce Tony to.

Two days? I'd lost track of everything except our mission.

"I want to go, to the beach and to the opening," Adriana said. "We'll have a ball. It's a pity there's only one swell left to make sheep's eyes at you, but who knows who might turn up. We should be famous now."

Heat rose in my cheeks. "Nobody is making sheep's eyes at me, and we're not famous."

196

CHAPTER TWENTY-SIX

"**Y**ou're famous." Jolene had used the back door to escape an especially tenacious young bespectacled man who clutched a stenographer's pad. He'd been camped outside for so long I'd called the café to order a muffin and coffee delivery for him.

"That is," she added with a self-satisfied gloat, "we are. I've been interviewed twice while I was changing locks."

"You've been pestered at work?" Aimée, who'd taken to Jolene in a flash, bristled.

"Not quite. I told them I'd only talk if I kept my hands busy." Jolene guffawed. "Rush job means twice the going rate. And I've got three more booked for tomorrow."

"Cobblewood Cove must be a hotbed of journalism," I marveled.

"They're from everywhere," Jolene said. "Which reminds me to add travel costs for out of city limits to my invoices."

Tony ventured closer, his tablet in his hand. Like most mature people, he struggled with reading longer texts on his phone. Unlike most, he readily admitted it. "It's online," he said.

"Let me see." Jolene peered over his shoulder and read aloud, "I could hear him threatening Genie Darling's life, and I knew I had to do something. When I jumped out of my hiding-place, he froze. His eyes bulged as if he'd seen a ghost. Nice touch that, eh?"

"She couldn't have seen his eyes," Adriana said under her breath. "Not with me taking care of the lights, thank you very much."

Jolene went on, "Asked how Ms Darling and she had come to suspect Mr Harewood, she said, There were a few red flags, but more details would have to wait until the trial. Her modesty and helpfulness, which have made her one of the most popular citizens of Cobblewood Cove, blah blah blah . . ." She held her hand up for a high five. "I thought if I give them a little something, they'll stop pestering you."

"And you get extra business at double the usual rate."

"It's not as if they have to hire me," Jolene said.

"I think you're doing a great job," Aimée told her. "Do you take on bigger projects as well? If we want to use this place as a more permanent base, we need to bring it up to 21st century standards. Lottie's wallpaper has to go."

Adriana agreed. "It's been making me cross-eyed." She shuddered. "Tell her to ask me first for approval though. I'm the one who's based here permanently."

I said nothing. I couldn't with all these witnesses hanging about.

I also kept my tongue when I trailed behind my mother and Tony for the Schuylers' big moment. By now, there were no more revelations expected from the reporters, so I could hide in the background and instead watch Dahlia, Primrose and Aimée holding court.

Adriana's coat hung around my great-great-aunt's shoulders.

In its place, a stovepipe hat with possible connections to President Lincoln in his lesser days garnered a few weak oohs and aahs.

The pièce de resistance turned out to be a chandelier made by Louis Tiffany, which had until now graced the Schuylers' family dining room. It had been removed last minute, to Petey's obvious distress, if the bird droppings were anything to go by.

Anything to do with the disgraced name of Jonathan Harewood had been removed and put into storage.

"It's not fair," Adriana said.

"What isn't?" I bit my tongue as Matt gave me a curious glance.

I lowered my voice. "Leave it to my mother to make sure that Tommy and Belle will be remembered as heroes."

Someone bumped into me and backed off as far as he could as Adriana hissed "Booh" at him.

Matt gave me another puzzled glance.

I gave up.

"I'll see you later," I signaled Tony.

He gave me a thumbs-up and returned his attention to Aimée who milked her glory as the center of attention. Coming home after decades and being the heiress to a fortune, plus a murder case straight out of the history books made her everyone's darling, as George put it.

I wondered how I could ever have suspected him, or Fred Ward. They both showered Aimée with enough attention to make aa lesser man than Tony nervous. Or Dahlia and Primrose jealous. After all, they'd worked hard to make this exhibition happen, and then Aimée swooped in and stole the limelight.

To their eternal credit, the two ladies watched my mother swan around in an evening dress that shimmered softly with every moment, and Belle's rediscovered necklace around her throat. Tony and Matt had arranged for insurance, and Adriana's set now had been officially gifted to me. That saved me from coaxing them out of my mother. I needed those gems.

"Are you leaving so soon?" Matt asked as I stole towards the exit.

"I could ask you the same," I said, since he too made for the door.

He fell into lockstep with me, to Adriana's delight. Her love for Cary Grant, which she'd cemented with repeat viewing of *Topper* when I'd believed I had to prepare her for the joys of her next phase, didn't stop her from appreciating flesh and blood men, or rather, a flesh and blood Matt.

He waited until we were at my doorstep to spring a surprise on me. "If you're free for dinner tomorrow, I'd like to take you out. Last chance for me."

For no reason, my heart beat a little louder. "Right, your job here is done."

"Yeah. Fun while it lasted, but . . ."

"What's next?"

"Another work trip. To Europe, this once."

"That's amazing."

"We'll see. Dahlia and Primrose have discovered a note in one of the letters they were given, about a trunk full of donated clothes and jewels that were shipped to Europe with a local girl who'd won a scholarship to Oxford." He rubbed this chin. "Come to think of it, it was one of your family letters. Anyway, this young lady went on to become a renowned scientist and she married into the aristocracy. Her estate has now come up for auction, and the Schuylers are keen on bringing home anything of value to the museum."

Clothes and jewelry! My eyes came close to popping out of my sockets. "Do you have any idea when this trunk was sent?"

He averted his gaze. "Soon after the two Darling girls passed away. Lots of people do that, give away things they can't bear to see any longer and yet can't dispose of."

Adriana stared at me with naked longing.

"Europe," I said. "That's rather vague."

"It's two lots they're after. One auction is in England, the other is on the continent, I'd have to check again. Do you want me to see if there's anything related to your family?"

"Please," I said.

"Consider it done."

Adriana twirled around the hallway. "I told you he's the bee's knees. I'm going to have all my lovely dresses back, and Belle's too."

"If I can afford them."

"You're not behind the eight ball, are you?"

"I'm also not rich."

"But they're mine." True. And she needed them.

"Matt can tell everyone, they're fake, like with the goggles."

"That won't work, but we'll come up with something. Only make sure you really really know which things we want."

"Oh, sure. And how exactly do you expect me to do that?"

"Like you said, duck soup." I relished the surprised expression on her face. Unless I'd remembered her slang wrong and it didn't mean what I thought it meant. "Should be easy enough if you use your eyes."

The unspoken words "She's loopy", hung in the air. I could have sworn I saw Cleo roll her eyes. I decided to play it cool.

"Unless you want to stay here," I said. "That's up to you. I, on the other hand, am booked to sail to Europe in a week. It's not the Queen Elizabeth II, or the Titanic…"

"That one sank," she pointed out.

"But nevertheless, I shall be on board and pay for my ticket with giving lessons in basic jewelry making. I could pack a few bricks if you want to tag along."

"Europe." She sank to the ground in a sweeping motion any movie director would have hired her for. "I've never been further than Niagara Falls. Where are we going? Paris? London? Vienna?"

"Wherever we need to go."

She floated in the air with happiness. "I want to see Josephine Baker."

"Too late. But some of her old haunts are still around."

"Then are we waiting for? We should be packing." Adriana showered Cleo's head with kisses. "You and me and Genie makes three. It'll be the best fun ever."

Adriana dance, Cleo purred, and I only hoped the cat would have the good sense to keep quiet about her staying home.

Adriana should be able to live her best life while she could. That meant we would not go around breaking her heart. The only real hitch I saw, though, was her dependence on me being the damsel in distress.

I'd have to stock up on books about the perils at sea. I mentally rolled up my sleeves. I had a lot to do, but whatever the future held, it was bound to be interesting.

The lights came on and went out in a flash. Maybe I wouldn't have to worry about telling Adriana stories about dangers ahead.

Wherever she was, became a fraught place. I wondered if Faraday's cage worked for a ghost. Or what else I could do to constrain my great-great-aunt.

Cleo gazed at me in what I took to be full understanding. Adriana had to be held in check. Except - where was she?

"Don't dawdle." An arm poked through the wall and beckoned me.

Great.

Now she could walk through walls.

What had I let myself in for?

***

A note from Carmen Radtke:

Have ghost. Will travel.

If her old belongings are vital for Adriana's continued existence (or passing over to another plane), Genie is more than happy to travel with her great-great-aunt to an auction in Italy.

But when an arsonist torches the auction house and kills a man in the process, all their hopes of buying back Adriana's precious things turn to ashes.

Still, Genie and her spectral pet-whispering sidekick are intent to keep the flames of justice burning and bring the killer into the open daylight ...

The sleuthing double-act returns in Ghost Takes A Vacation, the second novel in this fun-filled paranormal cozy mystery series full of unforgettable characters!

Preorder Ghost Takes A Vacation now for more criminally spooky action.

About the Author

Carmen has spent most of her life with ink on her fingers, cozy crime plots on her mind (thank you, Agatha Christie) and a dangerously high pile of books and newspapers by her side.

She has worked as a newspaper reporter on two continents and always dreamt of becoming a novelist and screenwriter.

When she found herself crouched under her dining table, typing away on a novel between two earthquakes in Christchurch, New Zealand, she realised she was hooked for life.

The shaken but stirring novel made it to the longlist of the Mslexia competition, and her next book and first mystery, The Case Of The Missing Bride, was a finalist in the Malice Domestic competition in a year without a winner. Since then she has penned several more cozy mysteries, including the Jack and Frances series set in the 1930s.

Genie and the Ghost is the first in a series of fun-filled paranormal cozy mysteries.

In real life, Carmen is absolutely law-abiding, has never met a ghost or been able to communicate with pets (sad, but true). The only time she shed blood and swatted a fly was by accident.

Her wanderlust has led her to live in Germany, New Zealand, and the UK. She currently lives in Italy with her human and her four-legged family.

If you want to keep in touch with her and find out more about her work, writing life, and other related things, sign up for her newsletter on her website www.carmenradtke.com and receive a free quick read!

You can also follow her on Amazon, BookBub and Facebook.

Also by Carmen Radtke

The Jack and Frances cozy 1930s mysteries
A Matter of Love and Death
Murder at the Races
Murder Makes Waves
Death Under Palm Trees
The Mystery of the Christmas Bauble (a quick read)
The Case of the Christmas Angel (a quick read)

The Alyssa Chalmers Victorian mysteries
The Case of the Missing Bride
The Prospect of Death
The Tunnels of Doom (coming in 2024)

The cozy contemporary Eve Holdsworth mysteries
Let Sleeping Murder Lie
A Dash of Deceit
Death at the Dog Show
Death on the Airwaves (coming in October 2023)

Stand-alone novels
Dig Your Own Grave
Walking in the Shadow